THE OFFICE GRAPEVINE

Barrington Corporation News Bulletin
Vol.1 No. 3
March

• Rumors abound about Molly Doyle and her sexy boss, Jack Cavanaugh. The latest news is that Molly has lost her memory and thinks she is married to the high-powered businessman. Close friends of the pair say this charade may lead to the real thing....

• Congratulations to Sophia Shepherd. She's been named executive secretary to Rex Barrington III. However, the mystery surrounding "The Third" continues—we hear even Sophia still has no idea what the man looks like!

• And, did anyone know Rachel Sinclair was almost engaged to her boss? Unfortunately, he was transferred and didn't propose before leaving. But Cupid may get the chance to strike again—confidential sources say Nick Delaney is under consideration as the new director of accounting and may return to Barrington....

Dear Reader,

March roars in like a lion at Silhouette Romance, starting with popular author Susan Meier and *Husband from 9 to 5,* her exciting contribution to LOVING THE BOSS, a six-book series in which office romance leads to happily-ever-after. In this sparkling story, a bump on the head has a boss-loving woman believing she's married to the man of her dreams....

In March 1998, beloved author Diana Palmer launched VIRGIN BRIDES. This month, *Callaghan's Bride* not only marks the anniversary of this special Romance promotion, but it continues her wildly successful LONG, TALL TEXANS series! As a rule, hard-edged, hard-bodied Callaghan Hart distrusted sweet, virginal, starry-eyed young ladies. But ranch cook Tess Brady had this cowboy hankerin' to break all his rules.

Judy Christenberry's LUCKY CHARM SISTERS miniseries resumes with a warm, emotional pretend engagement story that might just lead to *A Ring for Cinderella.* When a jaded attorney delivers a very pregnant stranger's baby, he starts a journey toward healing...and making this woman his *Texas Bride,* the heartwarming new novel by Kate Thomas. In *Soldier and the Society Girl* by Vivian Leiber, the month's HE'S MY HERO selection, sparks fly when a true-blue, true-grit American hero requires the protocol services of a refined blue blood. A lone-wolf lawman meets his match in an indomitable schoolteacher—and her moonshining granny—in Gayle Kaye's *Sheriff Takes a Bride,* part of FAMILY MATTERS.

Enjoy this month's fantastic offerings, and make sure to return each and every month to Silhouette Romance!

Mary-Theresa Hussey

Mary-Theresa Hussey
Senior Editor, Silhouette Romance

Please address questions and book requests to:
Silhouette Reader Service
U.S.: 3010 Walden Ave., P.O. Box 1325, Buffalo, NY 14269
Canadian: P.O. Box 609, Fort Erie, Ont. L2A 5X3

HUSBAND
FROM 9 TO 5

Susan Meier

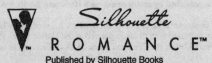

V Silhouette

R O M A N C E™

Published by Silhouette Books

America's Publisher of Contemporary Romance

Special thanks and acknowledgment are given
to Linda Susan Meier for her contribution to the
Loving the Boss series.

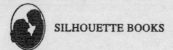 SILHOUETTE BOOKS

ISBN 0-373-19354-8

HUSBAND FROM 9 TO 5

Copyright © 1999 by Harlequin Books S.A.

This edition published by arrangement with Harlequin Books S.A.

® and TM are trademarks of Harlequin Books S.A., used under license.
Trademarks indicated with ® are registered in the United States Patent
and Trademark Office, the Canadian Trade Marks Office and in other
countries.

Printed in U.S.A.

Books by Susan Meier

Silhouette Romance

Stand-in Mom #1022
Temporarily Hers #1109
Wife in Training #1184
Merry Christmas, Daddy #1192
In Care of the Sheriff #1283
Guess What? We're Married! #1338
Husband From 9 to 5 #1354

*Texas Family Ties

Silhouette Desire

Take the Risk #567

SUSAN MEIER

is the author of eight category romances. A full-time employee of a major defense contractor, Susan has also been a columnist for a small newspaper and a division manager of a charitable organization. But her greatest joy in life has always been her children, who constantly surprise and amaze her. Married for twenty years to her wonderful, understanding and gorgeous husband, Michael, Susan cherishes her roles as mother, wife, sister and friend, believing them to be life's real treasures. She tries to convey the beauty and importance of loving relationships in her books.

VERY IMPORTANT MESSAGE

For _Molly_

From _Your Mother_

Phone _____

TELEPHONED	✓	PLEASE CALL	✓
CALLED TO SEE YOU		WILL CALL AGAIN	
WANTS TO SEE YOU		URGENT	✓
	RETURNED YOUR CALL		

Message _Your parents heard a rumor that you're married to your boss and they want to know if it's true -- especially since no one even knew you were dating Jack Cavanaugh !!)_

Chapter One

"Aren't you coming?"

Molly Doyle peered up from the ad she was revising to see her boss—tall, dark, and devastating Jack Cavanaugh, director of advertising for Barrington Corporation—standing in her doorway.

With both hands braced on the door frame above his head, Jack easily filled the empty space. His olive green plaid suit coat hung open, revealing his plain green tie and the white shirt that hugged his broad chest and trim waist. His dark brown hair was ruffled enough for Molly to know he'd probably combed his fingers through it a time or two during the course of the gruelling afternoon. The untidy waves boyishly tipped to his forehead, accenting serious brown eyes that sparkled with warmth.

Molly just barely checked a sigh of appreciation. "Yes, I'm coming," she said, pronouncing every word carefully to keep herself from stammering because the man was simply too sexy for a sane woman to remain composed when she was in the same room with him. But Molly was in even worse shape than the average sane woman. She'd worked with Jack for over four years and in that time had fallen hopelessly in love with him. He wasn't merely an attractive man to Molly. No, to Molly Doyle Jack Cavanaugh was perfect. Just looking at him made her weak-kneed.

Unfortunately, not once in four years had she detected that she had the same effect on him. If the truth were known, Molly would have to admit she didn't seem to stir up any kind of feelings in him at all—which was why she carefully hid hers. He had breakfasts, lunches and dinners with nearly everyone in their department. Most people considered him a confidante. But Molly had yet to have anything beyond a superficial conversation with him. Some of her friends hypothesized that that might be because he had feelings for her, too, and didn't know how to show them so he was afraid to be alone with her. Others thought she and Jack weren't close in the way the rest of her department was because she didn't have any problems for Jack to solve. The final few figured Jack was thick-skulled and bullheaded, and if anyone was going to make the first move, it would have to be Molly.

"I'll be there in a minute. I wanted to take one last peek at..."

"Uh-uh-uh," Jack said, and strode behind her chair. Before Molly realized what he was about to do, he pulled her seat out from under her desk. When it was free, he grabbed her arms and forced her to stand. "I said no one works late tonight. We're going to Mahoney's. Drinks are on me, remember?"

Little pinpricks of awareness radiated outward from the places Jack touched. For the next ten seconds Molly was lucky to remember her name, let alone the plans Jack had made for tonight's celebration. She took a minute to regain her equilibrium by clearing her throat. "Yes, I remember."

"Good. Get your jacket," Jack said, and headed for her

door. But he stopped suddenly. "You do have a ride, don't you?"

She was tempted, sorely tempted, to tell him no, if only to test out everybody's theories. If she told him she didn't have her car, he'd undoubtedly invite her to go with him. Then he'd have to take her home. And maybe, just maybe...

She shook her head as if clearing a haze. She had her car. If she left it here, she wouldn't have a ride to work in the morning. Besides, he knew she drove a little white Lexus, a gift from her parents. If he spotted it as they were walking toward his Blazer, he'd know she lied, and she'd blow everything because she couldn't see wholesome, honest, honorable Jack Cavanaugh marrying a liar—no matter how good her intentions.

"I have my car. This way if I want to leave early—"

"No one's leaving early," Jack interrupted, grinning. "This is a celebration. It was incredible that we got that magazine layout in on time. We all deserve a night out. And tonight's the night."

"Yeah, well, tomorrow's still Thursday," Molly said briskly. Needing a minute to recover from the effects of that grin, she turned away from him to gather her jacket and purse from the coat tree beside her putty-colored filing cabinet. "And some of us work better with eight hours of sleep," she added, meeting Jack at the doorway.

Jack motioned for her to precede him, then flicked off her office lights. "So sleep in. I don't expect to see anybody working in this department before ten tomorrow morning."

"But Mr. Barrington—"

"Gave me complete control of this department," Jack said, finishing her sentence. "If he has a question, he'll come to me and I'll explain. That's what bosses are for."

He punctuated his sentence with a light tap on the tip of her nose, and it was then—right in that second—that Molly realized her fantasy of someday marrying Jack Cavanaugh was absolutely pointless. In a sudden flash of insight, she saw that the tap personified exactly how he felt about her. He treated her like a kid. Specifically he treated her like an errant younger cousin. She and her friends hadn't figured that out because they didn't want to. Each and every one of them *wanted* to believe Jack Cavanaugh was the man of her dreams. So—in various and sundry forms, modifications and excuses—that's what they saw.

But the truth wasn't quite so romantic. After over four years of working together, Jack Cavanaugh still judged her as too young to even be his friend. There was no way he was *ever* going to see her as a peer, let alone a woman or a lover.

By treating her like a kid, Jack as good as told her there would never be anything between them.

In a sense she had just been dumped.

Because Jack went back to his office for his briefcase, he and Molly parted company before they reached the elevator. Crushed by her realization, Molly sighed heavily as she strode across the parking lot of Barrington Corporation toward her car, not even noticing the sweet scent of the spring air or the warmth characteristic of March in Phoenix. The weather was mild enough that she didn't need to put her all-weather coat over her fawn-colored silk blouse and brushed denim trousers. It hung limply over her arm, as lifeless and listless as she felt.

When she reached her Lexus, she opened her door and jumped inside. But two seconds before her coat would have covered the latest package from her parents, Molly stopped it.

She knew what was in the box. Tapes. Her parents were Dominic and Darcy Doyle—success coaches, business gurus, the king and queen of self-help and infomercials. Every time they cut a new tape, they sent the first copy to her. And every time they sent her a new tape, they expected her life to turn around overnight.

She didn't have the heart to tell them that she hadn't even listened to the set of tapes that made them their first million, but she suspected they knew it from the fact that she was still a copywriter in the advertising department for Barrington— the same job she landed right out of college. There was no way she could explain to two supermotivated motivationalists that she simply had no desire to someday rule the world. What she wanted more than anything else was to be a mother. Once she met Jack Cavanaugh, she thought her fate had been sealed. Cupid's arrow hit its mark and she fell head over heels in love with a man with the body of a Greek god, the compassion, patience and kindness of a saint, and the warmth and personality of the boy next door. One look at Jack and she knew her dreams of home and hearth were right on target. This was the man with whom she was destined to share her life. This was the man with whom she was destined to raise her five children. She knew it as surely as her parents knew that time management was essential to goal setting. It was almost as if a picture had formed in her head, and she could see Jack, their five kids and even bits and pieces of what their house would look like.

She hadn't confided to her parents that being an only child had caused her to long for home and family. It wasn't her intention to make them feel guilty. It wasn't even Molly's intention to fill a void. Her desire was more like a quest, like a destiny. If the world still needed a new ruler after her kids were in college, well, then, maybe she'd give her parents' tapes a try. But for now—at least for the past four years— her heart, her soul, her every waking minute had been committed to the dream of marrying Jack Cavanaugh.

The only problem was, she'd failed.

In fact, if this afternoon's encounter was any indicator, Molly would have to admit she hadn't merely failed, she'd never been in the ball game.

Sighing again, Molly picked up the box, then smiled. Her

mother had added the easy-pull string. One yank on the strategically placed strand and the box would be open. Her parents were so predictable...but in a good way. And, frankly, all they ever really wanted was for Molly to be happy. Unfortunately, to her parents, happiness translated into promotions, material possessions and a certain amount of fame. They worried about her because she didn't get promotions, she lived in a cheerful, but tiny, apartment, her car was only top of the line because it had been a gift from them, and—as for fame—she didn't have any. No one, absolutely no one, knew who she was. People didn't recognize her as the daughter of the supersuccessful Doyles. Doyle was such a common name, no one knew she was the sole heir to a small fortune.

In a sense she understood why her parents worried about her. Maybe she was even starting to agree with them. After this afternoon she realized she was nothing but a silly dreamer. Jack Cavanaugh wasn't ever going to see her as anything more than his copywriter. She wasn't ever going to have his babies. It was time she forgot that foolish daydream and got on with the rest of her life.

Chewing her bottom lip, she yanked on her mother's easy-open string and opened the box. The smooth vinyl case inside read Think Your Way to the Top by Dominic and Darcy Doyle. Her parents' faces smiled at her from beneath the title. She could have sworn that when she perforated the plastic wrapper, her mother winked.

Without further thought, Molly extracted tape one, entitled "See It, Be It" and popped it into her tape deck.

When Jack Cavanaugh entered Mahoney's, he scanned the dimly lit bar, searching for Molly. God only knew what had gotten into her over the past few weeks, but something was wrong. He'd come to depend on Molly for much, much more than copywriting, and just as he was on the verge of asking her to take the position as his assistant and giving her total control over certain areas of their department, something happened. She couldn't seem to concentrate at meetings anymore. She didn't seem all that interested in their work. Then, this afternoon, when he gave everyone the opportunity to take a break, suddenly all she wanted to do was work.

Something was wrong. He knew it. But unlike everyone else in their department, she'd never allowed him to get close enough to her that she would confide in him. But tonight that was going to change. Tonight he planned on sticking to her like glue, until she was comfortable enough that she would break down and tell him her problem. Then, big brother that he prided himself on being, Jack would help her solve her dilemma and all would be right with the world again.

The six members of Barrington's advertising department had already assembled at a table in the corner, but Jack strode to the bar to order three pizzas and to make arrangements to pay for anything bought by anyone in his group. Then he ordered a pitcher of beer, gathered a few extra glasses and headed for the table.

"Hey, boss," Bryce Patterson, the short, bald ad man said, as he rose to relinquish his seat at the head of the table. "You sit here."

"No, no. This is fine," Jack argued, taking the chair beside the department receptionist, Julie Cramer. Julie was a tall, sultry brunette, who always had trouble with her boyfriend. Tonight Jack would probably spend a few minutes counseling her on what to do to keep her relationship intact, so he decided he might as well get that done early. Particularly since he wanted plenty of time for Molly. Wherever she was.

"That was a great campaign we finished this afternoon," Jack said, pausing when he heard the front door open. He glanced over his shoulder, saw a man in his early twenties sauntering to the bar and faced his group again. "It was nothing short of a miracle that we finished the magazine segment this afternoon and got it off before deadline. Mr. Barrington will be thrilled.''

"I'm just glad to be done,'' Bryce said, hoisting his glass as if in a toast. The other members of the department agreed by raising their glasses, too.

Jack also raised his glass, but hastily glanced behind him when the door opened again. Two women in their early thirties entered, probably stopping for dinner, but no Molly.

Where the hell was she? She'd left a good ten minutes before he did. They would have taken the same route. So how did he get here before her?

Jack was on the verge of guessing that she'd chosen not to join the department for this celebration when she walked through the door. She brought the fading rays of the day's sunlight with her and, shrouded in the light as she was, Jack had the impression that he was looking at an angel. Light glistened off her shoulder-length blond hair, her hazel eyes sparkled. To see the ethereal vision standing in the doorway, with her strangely contented smile, he would have never known this was the same woman he'd been so worried about. She was perfect. Happy. Healthy. Tall, thin, beautiful. Incredibly beautiful.

Shaking his head at the unexpected turn of his thoughts, Jack rose from his seat to signal for her to join them. She gave him an odd smile, and almost seemed to hesitate, but then she picked up her pace and walked to the table.

"Hi, everyone.''

"Hey, Molly,'' Bryce said, and pulled out the chair beside him for her to sit down. "Where were you?''

Jack didn't know why he was so curious, but he was. In fact, he was inordinately glad Bryce had asked the question.

"I went home at lunch to pick up my mail, and I had gotten a package from my parents. So I thought I'd open it before I drove over.''

"What was it? Cookies?" Sandy Johnson, the department secretary, asked with a laugh.

"No," Molly said, accepting the glass of beer Bryce had poured for her. "My parents aren't exactly the cookies type."

"What type are they?" Rick Ingells asked, obviously interested. As far as Jack could tell, Rick, one of Barrington's accountants, was the only out-of-department guest at this party. He wasn't sure who had invited him and, with Rick's sudden attention to Molly's parents, Jack wasn't sure he was glad the green-eyed, tall-dark-and-handsome accountant had joined them.

"They're more the computer, E-mail, fax and modem type."

"Oh, computer nerds," Julie said dispassionately.

Molly shook her head. "No, more the be-all-that-you-can-be type."

"Army?" Bryce asked, confused.

Molly laughed heartily. "No. My parents are professional success consultants. They help people transform their lives."

"Sounds boring," Julie said.

"You know, I thought so until tonight," Molly said, her gaze colliding with Jack's, then skittering away again. "But tonight I'm kind of thinking that they're on to something." She glanced around once, quickly, then changed the subject. "Anybody order the pizza yet? I don't want to drink on an empty stomach."

In spite of the way Molly switched topics, Jack hadn't missed that slip. Molly's problem seemed to have something to do with her parents. From the sounds of things, she might have had a running disagreement with them, but because of whatever it was they sent her in the mail she was starting to see things their way. Which was probably why she seemed happy. Ending a disagreement always brought a sense of relief. Coming to that conclusion, Jack wondered if he even needed to talk with Molly about her problems, then he deter-

mined that he was going to stick with his first impression.
She was the only member of his staff with whom he didn't
have a close, personal, big-brother type relationship. Tonight
was the night he planned to work toward getting one.

For the next twenty minutes Jack's time was taken by Julie
whose boyfriend was having a great deal of trouble keeping
a job. Molly listened, almost jealously, as Jack guided her
through steps that would assist her in helping her boyfriend
pinpoint his best career options. But as the night wore on, as
the pizza came and was eaten, Molly realized that Jack's ability to be such a good friend to everyone in his department
was part of what she loved about him.

And she did *love* him. There wasn't a soul on this earth
who could tell her she didn't. After more than four years of
working with him, she knew her feelings.

"Pool, Molly?" Bryce asked, handing her a stick.

She shrugged and rose. "Sure, why not?"

Walking around the table gave her plenty of opportunities
to look at Jack without him knowing she was studying him.
This was her big decision night. Whether her parents intended
to or not, they'd given her the clue to the rest of her life.
After listening to their tape Molly realized she could take their
strategies and bolster her professional life, or she could take
their strategies and give one last effort to making her real
dream—marrying Jack Cavanaugh—come true.

Now all she had to do was choose her direction.

Even as preoccupied as she was, Molly handily beat Bryce.
But she didn't really want to play pool. She wanted to make
a decision. When Jack rose and offered to play the next game,
she deftly relinquished her stick.

She wasn't exactly sure, but as she headed back to the table
she thought she heard Jack swear under his breath.

After Bryce broke, then missed his next shot, Jack made a
production number out of taking his first shot, strutting

around the table, analyzing the lay of the balls. Gnawing her bottom lip, Molly watched him. He'd removed his suit coat, unbuttoned the top button of his white shirt, loosened his tie and rolled his sleeves to his elbows. The light from the low-hanging fixture above the pool table threw shadows across his handsome face, making him appear outrageously sexy. If Molly didn't already know that the heart of a wonderful, generous, compassionate man beat in his powerful chest, she probably would have thought him a rogue. He simply had the looks for it. Dark. Forbidding. So sexy, her heart skipped a beat.

Right then and there she made her decision. She was going for it. Darn it. Her parents' tapes boldly proclaimed that if she could see it, she could be it. They clearly stated that if she could visualize herself achieving her dream, she would achieve it.

Well, her dream wasn't to climb a corporate ladder, which was the typical goal of the audience they planned to reach. But her dream wasn't any more ridiculous than a mail room clerk wishing to become company president.

And she was at a crossroad. Instinct told her it was now or never. So, ridiculous as it might seem, she was going to visualize. If her parents were right, all she had to do was create a scenario in her head that manifested the four most important steps to achieving her goal. To Molly that meant she first had to conjure a scenario where Jack would actually notice her as a woman. Then she'd have to envision what their first date would be like. Then she'd have to see their first sexual encounter. Then, finally, she'd have to imagine her wedding day.

Still uncertain, she glanced over at the pair at the pool table, Bryce and Jack. Unexpectedly, she caught Jack's gaze and he smiled, then winked.

Well, if that wasn't confirmation that she should go for it, Molly didn't know what was.

She returned his smile tentatively, took a deep breath, then leaned back on her chair. Though her eyes were open, she focused on the pictures forming in her brain.

She concluded that if Jack was ever going to notice her as a woman, it wouldn't be at the office. No. They had too much history there. If he hadn't seen her as a woman in that setting, he never would. So, in her mind she reasoned that he had to come to her apartment to drop off a file. She would open the door wearing only pajamas and her pink satin robe—another gift from her parents. At first Jack would be uncomfortable, but soon Molly would realize that his discomfort wasn't from being at her home, but rather from her scanty outfit.

She wasn't sure it was appropriate to make her visualization so risqué, but the first time a man notices a woman as a *woman,* things would be a little heated, so there really was no way around it. Maybe it was time to jump to the first date?

Okay. Jack sees her as a woman, so he asks her out. They have a nice, quiet dinner at a dark, moody restaurant. Everything goes smoothly. They laugh. They talk about deep, personal subjects. And when they settle in Jack's car to go home, Jack reaches over and pulls her to him for a kiss. But just the touch of his mouth on hers sets her lips on fire, and before she knows what's happening they're both drawn into a whirlwind of passion. Their tongues entwine. His hand accidentally brushes across her breast....

Yikes! That had tipped toward X-rated.

Taking a deep breath, Molly brought herself back to the present in time to see Jack striding toward the table. He walked to her seat, placed his hand on her shoulder and, gazing directly into her eyes, said, "Why don't you and I shoot a game of pool?"

Molly could have sworn her heart stopped. It was the first time in four years he'd touched her so intimately. He'd touched her to get her attention, to help her stand or to make a point, but he'd never touched her while gazing into her eyes, particularly not when his eyes held a special glow that drew her in and created a sort of intimacy between them. If she didn't know better, Molly might think her visualizations were reaching him telepathically.

Or maybe her parents were right. Maybe in visualizing, she was beginning to see things that were always there but that she never acknowledged because her own inhibitions were preventing her from believing what she considered to be impossible.

She cleared her throat, ready to take Jack up on his offer, but Julie Cramer interrupted. "I want to play pool," she said, whining.

In that second, it seemed as if time stopped. Molly peeked at Jack. Jack sent a smoldering glance to Molly. He gave her a look that told Molly in no uncertain terms that the night wasn't over for them.

Her breath caught.

Jack faced Julie.

"Sure. You and I can play a game, but next time around, Molly and I play."

"Yeah, right, whatever," Julie said, rising from her seat to walk to the pool table.

Molly almost fanned herself. That was the closest, the absolute closest, she and Jack had ever come to a personal encounter. And though it seemed utterly ridiculous, Molly had nothing to credit for this turn of events except her visualization.

Wild horses couldn't have kept her from completing her experiment now.

Deciding that the train of her thoughts was too unruly to handle imagining their first sexual encounter, Molly skipped ahead to imagining their wedding. First, she carefully chose her gown. White satin, sequins, seed pearls and a twenty-five-foot Italian lace train—what was the point in having rich parents if she couldn't have a great gown? Then she visualized

Jack in a trim black tux. His white shirt would have black onyx studs for buttons. His slightly curly brown hair would be perfect that day. His eyes would hold a mysterious, devilish shine that would send her messages the whole way through the ceremony.

They'd have the reception in the Beverly Hills Regency. And she'd indulge her parents by letting them invite every person they knew. The ballroom would be filled to capacity with smiling well-wishers, but she and Jack would only have eyes for each other....

"Care to dance?"

Even with the light tap on her shoulder, Jack's interruption startled Molly so much, she nearly gasped.

She drew a shuddering breath to regain her equilibrium and twisted on her chair to look at him. Again his eyes held that odd shine. His expression took her right back to their wedding. The Italian lace. The Regency. And the look that held so much promise...

"Dance?" she croaked, abruptly yanking herself out of her fantasy because she was starting to confuse it with reality. "I thought we were going to play pool?"

He grinned sheepishly. "I lost the pool table. Two hustlers from the bar took me for three bucks and got control of the table when they beat me."

Molly couldn't help it; she smiled. He was so damned cute when he was embarrassed. And they were going to *dance*. Not play pool. She didn't know what magic there was in visualization, but whatever it was, it was working. Any day of the week, dancing was preferable to playing pool. The force was definitely with her.

"I'd love to dance."

Jack took her hand and guided her toward the small section near the jukebox—between the pool table and the bar—that had been cordoned off for dancing. Two other couples huddled together, swaying to the music, so Molly didn't feel the least bit uncomfortable. She also noticed that she must have daydreamed most of the night away because everyone from the advertising department had disappeared—probably gone home.

Which was even better, Molly determined, as Jack pulled her into his arms. Now she didn't have to worry about anyone gossiping.

Content, Molly snuggled against Jack's shoulder and simply enjoyed. He was warm, he was strong, he was everything a woman could want in a man. If she were going to visualize being married to him, cuddled in his arms was exactly where she'd want to do it.

Mrs. Jack Cavanaugh, she thought, using the name like an affirmation, another trick from her parents' tapes. They believed that if you wanted something, all you had to do was say it aloud, as if it were real, and eventually it would be real.

Mrs. Jack Cavanaugh. She thought it again, this time smiling, thinking about their life together, their kids and the million memories they'd make in a lifetime.

Mrs. Jack Cavanaugh...

In the middle of her last affirmation, a loud commotion broke out. Her thoughts disturbed, Molly moved away from Jack's shoulder and saw that the two men at the pool table were shouting obscenities at two men trying to make their way to the bar. Before she could fully comprehend what was happening, one of the pool hustlers leapt over the pool table, obviously intending to head off the two men striding toward the bar.

For Molly the scene played in slow motion. She saw the man leap over the table. She realized he'd jumped too hard and was coming toward her. She tried to get out of his way.

But it was too late.

Chapter Two

The jumper actually only grazed Molly, but he was moving with enough momentum that he knocked her off balance and she tumbled backward. As she fell, she bumped her head on a nearby table. Jack desperately attempted to catch her, but he failed and she dropped to the floor. Within seconds, the entire population of Mahoney's gathered around them.

"Oh my gosh! Molly," Jack said, sliding his arm under her shoulders so he could raise her head from the cold linoleum. "Molly!"

With everyone's attention centered on Molly, the pool player who had jumped over the table scrambled out the door. If Jack hadn't been so concerned about Molly, he probably would have darted after him. But right at this minute, his most important duty was taking care of Molly.

"Molly," he called again, urgently.

She moaned softly, then weakly said, "I'm all right."

Because Jack didn't think she'd been knocked unconscious, he breathed a sigh of relief. "Molly, can you sit up?"

"I'll get her a glass of water," the bartender volunteered and scurried away.

"I'll help you get her to a chair," one of the patrons said.

"Thanks," Jack said, but he easily lifted Molly himself and carried her to the closest seat, the crowd parting for him as he walked through.

"What happened?" she asked groggily as he sat her down.

"One of the guys playing pool pushed you and you fell," Jack said, hunkering down beside her chair. "You grazed your head on a table but I don't think you fainted."

"You don't?"

"No, I don't."

"Here's the water," the bartender said, handing Jack the tall glass.

Jack held it to Molly's lips. "Drink this."

She drank two small sips then turned her face away. "I'm fine."

"You're sure?" Jack asked skeptically. Because she hadn't taken too much of a fall, Jack knew she probably wasn't seriously injured, but she didn't seem like herself, either.

"Yeah, I'm okay."

Narrowing his eyes for a better look, Jack said, "You know what? You might be okay, but I think it would be a good idea if I drove you home tonight."

Molly gave him a blank stare. "Yeah. Right. Whatever."

Oddly enough, she sounded like Julie, the receptionist, and Jack winced. He'd heard stories about the power of suggestion and he'd hate to think that a bump on the noggin would change his supercompetent employee into an empty-headed whiner who thought only of herself.

After gathering Molly's purse and paying the tab, Jack guided her to his Blazer. Once he had her settled inside, he ran over to her car to make sure it was locked. As he suspected, detail-oriented Molly had taken all possible precautions to ensure the safety of her Lexus. Moving away, he patted the shiny white door and even spent a second admiring the beautiful pale leather interior, but as he hurried back to his Blazer it suddenly struck him that a Lexus was a very expensive car for a person who earned the salary he knew Molly earned.

He decided that was none of his business, opened his car door and jumped inside. "Still okay?" he asked, smiling over at Molly.

"Yeah. I'm fine."

Her speech wasn't slurred. Her eyes weren't overly bright or darkened by dilated pupils. She didn't appear nauseated. Clearing all those hurdles pretty much indicated that she didn't have a concussion. Still, Jack couldn't help but think something wasn't quite right. He simply couldn't put his finger on it.

"Buckle your seat belt," Jack said, then drove onto the street. From his peripheral vision, he noticed Molly had a little difficulty with the seat belt. But since he knew most people had trouble with that seat belt, he chose not to give that one thing more weight than it deserved. Unfortunately, when he got to the intersection and realized he didn't have a clue of where Molly lived, he glanced over and discovered Molly was sound asleep.

"Molly," he called softly.

She didn't answer.

He increased the volume slightly. "Molly?"

"What?" Her answer was gruff but strong. The fact that he could wake her meant she hadn't fainted, but fallen asleep. She didn't sound injured, merely tired. And why not? They'd killed themselves trying to get that layout out this afternoon.

Studying her angelic face, softened by sleep and bathed in the light of a street lamp, Jack knew he had two options. One, wake her and get her address. Two, take her to his house, let her get the rest she obviously needed and keep an eye on her through the night to be sure she truly was okay.

Actually, he liked the second option. She was tired. She

had been out of sorts for the last few weeks and she needed rest. And he sincerely did want to be sure she was okay.

Besides, he never did get the chance to have that heart-to-heart talk with her. In the morning, and in the privacy of his home, he was absolutely positive he could get her to open up to him. He'd also have the chance to offer her the job as his assistant.

He drove them to his house, turned his Blazer onto his driveway and waited the fifteen seconds it took for his garage door to open. Once his Blazer was parked, he jumped out, rounded the hood and helped Molly.

"Where are we?"

"My house. You're tired. You seem to need some rest, but more than that I'd like to keep an eye on you because of your fall."

She appeared to understand the logic in that and nodded. "Okay."

Well, that was easy, Jack thought, then led Molly through his semidark kitchen, down the hall and up the steps. The only bedroom of his four-bedroom house that had any furniture was his room, so he led Molly there, knowing he could be perfectly comfortable on his sofa because he'd slept there often enough. Holding her up by the side of the bed, he pulled down the covers, then helped her sit before he slid off her shoes.

"That's all the help I can give you," he said with a grin, indicating with a wave of his hand that he couldn't take off her silk blouse and brushed denim slacks. "There's a fresh toothbrush in the bathroom. I'll see you in the morning."

Less than eight hours later, soft kisses awakened Jack. It took a second for the recognition of what the warm, wet feeling was on the back of his neck, but once he realized what was happening, his eyes flew open and he swung around, nearly knocking Molly off the couch.

"Molly! What the hell are you doing?" he cried, scrambling to sit up on the sofa.

She smiled at him. "I'm waking you up, silly," she said, then reached for him again.

His eyes wide, Jack scurried out of her reach. "I think you've got the wrong idea here," he said, maneuvering himself over the back of the couch and completely out of harm's way. "I slept on the sofa all night...."

Molly's face scrunched up in confusion. "I know, and I can't remember why. Did we have a fight?"

For a good thirty seconds, Jack stared at her in complete confusion, his mouth hanging open. She looked so innocent, yet so sure of what she was saying, he felt like he'd missed a memo or a meeting or something. Cautious, he edged his way back to the sofa. "*We* didn't have a fight, but we sort of got caught in a fight at Mahoney's. You took a fall. I brought you home."

"Well, of course, you brought me home, silly. Where else would you take me? After six months of being married, I doubt that my parents would have me back." With that, Molly rose from the couch and headed for the kitchen.

Jack took a minute to digest that statement—wanting to be absolutely positive he'd heard what he'd heard—then he dashed after her, catching her by the white Formica counter that separated the eating area from the cooking area of his kitchen. "Whoa! Whoa! Wait a minute. What did you say?"

"I said my parents have a no-return policy, remember?" Molly said, then punctuated her statement with a quick kiss on his lips, as if she'd kissed him a hundred times. Jack fell to a stool by the counter. Molly headed for the refrigerator. "Eggs?"

"No, I don't want eggs!" Jack said, feeling that he was caught somewhere between a really, really good dream and a nightmare. "I want to know what the hell you're talking about."

"Remember how my parents have a no-return policy on their tapes?"

He didn't because he didn't know who the devil her parents were, but he figured he had to go along with this part of her explanation to get to the part he was interested in. "Yeah, I remember."

"Don't tell me you've already forgotten how we made that joke on our honeymoon that this marriage had better work because the Doyles have a no-return policy."

Jack's chest froze. *Honeymoon? Marriage?* What the hell was she talking about?

Standing by his refrigerator, still dressed in the clothing she'd worn the night before, one hand poised on her hip, Molly looked so crestfallen and so certain, that for a second Jack wondered if he'd lost his mind or his memory. But knowing that she was the one to get the bump on the head the night before he said, "Molly, we're not married."

"Very funny, Jack," she said, and stormed past him.

"Molly," Jack called, and darted after her. He caught her in the hallway and spun her around. After taking a breath to be sure he'd be gentle with her, he said, "Molly, you got a bump on the head last night. You *think* we're married...." He didn't have a clue why. "But we're not."

"I'm not in the mood for your silliness or your jokes today," she haughtily retorted, and headed for the steps. "I've got to get dressed for work."

Work! Good God! He'd be in trouble if she went into work thinking they were married.

Again he scrambled after her. "Wait! Molly, wait!"

She stopped on the stairway and peered down at him imperially. "Why? Ready to apologize?"

Jack almost said no and began another round of explanations, but he realized there was a more important issue here. If he couldn't convince her that they weren't married, he sure as hell couldn't let her go into their office.

"Yes," he said and started up the steps. "I apologize. I'm very sorry. Besides, I get the bathroom first today," he said taking her by the biceps. He brushed a quick, chaste kiss across her forehead and hoped it was convincing. "Because you don't have to go to work."

She wrinkled her nose. "I don't?"

"No," Jack said. "Remember, you fell last night at the bar and we concluded it would be best if you took a day off to rest?"

She shook her head. "No. I don't remember any of that."

Why was it that didn't surprise him? "Well that's what we decided. We decided that you were going to stay home from work today. So scoot. I need to use the bathroom."

When she continued to stare at him with a disbelieving expression, Jack smiled. "Or, if you wanted to be a good wife, you could make me some breakfast."

He struck a nerve. He knew it instantly because her eyes lit with joy and her lips curved upward into a dazzling smile.

"What would you like?"

He was tempted to say "the usual," if only to see what she'd come up with, but this was no time to push his luck. And he needed all the luck he could summon right now. He hoped that once he left for work Molly would go back to bed and when she awakened she'd be out of this delusion. Because if she wasn't, he was in big, big trouble.

"How about two eggs and some wheat toast?"

She stretched on her tiptoes and gave him a smacking kiss on the lips. "Two eggs and wheat toast it is," she said, and jogged down the steps.

Jack collapsed with relief then bounded up the remaining steps, had his shower and dressed as quickly as he could. He had two things to take care of this morning, but once those two things were handled, he was getting some help.

"She thinks you're what?"

"She thinks we're married."

A deafening silence followed Jack's statement. A pin drop in Barrington Corporation's break room would have sounded like a clap of thunder.

All Molly's closest friends were gathered. Patricia Peel, the strawberry blonde with light green eyes who worked as assistant personnel director. Cindy Cooper, a green-eyed brunette who'd recently gotten engaged to Kyle Prentice. Sophia Shepherd, a blue-eyed, blond secretary. Olivia McGovern-Hunter, the green-eyed, auburn-haired paralegal who had recently married Lucas Hunter. And Rachel Sinclair, a blue-eyed brunette accountant. Jack knew if anybody could help him figure out what to do with Molly, one of these women could.

The only problem was, nobody said a word.

"Our department went to Mahoney's last night to celebrate the fact that we got our magazine layout in on time," Jack said, filling the silence and hoping to say something that would entice someone into commenting. "I noticed Molly had been a little withdrawn all night, so after everybody had left, I asked her to dance."

Sophia raised her eyebrows. Rachel cleared her throat. Cindy disbelievingly said, "You what?"

"I asked her to dance. I wanted a chance to talk privately with her. But before we got three steps into the song, a hustler jumped over the pool table, trying to catch somebody heading for the bar, and he knocked into Molly. When she fell, she hit her head."

Again, dead silence. Five pair of eyes stared at him as if he were crazy or lying...or both.

Uncomfortable, but knowing he was going to have to explain even further, Jack leaned against the countertop. "She didn't pass out or anything and she said she was okay, but it was easy to talk her into letting me take her to my house."

"Your house?" Olivia gasped.

"Only to make sure she would be okay through the night."

As he was saying the last little bit, Julie Cramer, who had sauntered in a few minutes earlier, said, "Oh, that's a new one." She grabbed a can of diet soda then left the room again.

"What were you thinking, taking her to your house?" Olivia demanded, and unconsciously placed her palm on her rounding stomach. Jack heard the accusation as clearly as if she'd said it.

"Hey, she'd hit her head," Jack quickly explained. "I didn't want her driving. She fell asleep before she could give me her address. It all seemed logical at the time."

"Actually, it does," Patricia said, walking over to Jack. "You're lucky you have such a good reputation around here, otherwise, we'd wonder."

"Well, don't wonder. Help me. I don't know how the heck she got the cockamamie idea that we're married."

Olivia looked at Rachel, who looked at Patricia, who looked at Sophia, who looked at Cindy, who yelped, "Hey, I'm not saying anything!"

"About what?" Jack demanded suspiciously.

"About the fact that Molly has had a horrible crush on you for years," Olivia said, then drew a long breath. "If she thinks she's married to you, it's probably a combination of getting hit on the head, waking up in your bed...and her own fantasies."

"Oh, boy," Jack said, raking his fingers through his hair, not daring to dig too deeply into this because he wasn't sure he'd like what he'd find. "So, how do we get her out of it?"

"I think it might be better if you sort of stayed in the background, Jack," Sophia suggested. "If we all went over to your house right after work and explained things to Molly, she'd probably take it better coming from us."

"She might even get her real memory back simply from seeing us," Rachel added.

"Right. You're right," Jack agreed, and headed for the door. "I'll meet you all in the parking lot at four."

Chapter Three

Jack pulled his Blazer into his two-car garage and motioned for the vehicles containing Molly's co-workers to park in the driveway. He owned a large, two-story white frame house with cheerful forest green shutters. Full, bushy shrubs hunkered around the foundation. In front of them were smaller, more decorative varieties of perennials—flowers and plants Jack didn't need to plant every year, but which grew of their own accord. Because it was spring, they were beginning to blossom, making his home appear well tended and loved, in spite of the fact that he spent very little time there.

In the rear, bay windows overlooked a brick patio that ran from one end of the house to the other and edged a cement walkway that surrounded an in-ground pool—all of which was partially visible from the driveway because his garage doors were on the side of the house, not in front. Though no one made any comments, from their wide-eyed stares and curious glances, Jack could see Molly's friends were impressed. But for fifty cents Jack would have handed the key to any one of them.

He led them up the sidewalk to the beveled-glass front door, then let everybody inside the formal foyer.

"Molly," he called. "Molly."

Smiling brightly, she erupted from the kitchen like a small, blond tornado. She wore the same fawn-colored silk blouse from the night before with the matching brushed denim trousers, but today she'd covered both with the apron he used for grilling. The words The Next One To Complain Gets The Spatula were sprawled across her chest and torso.

"Darling, you're home," she said, and throwing her arms around his neck, kissed him soundly on the mouth. Every muscle in Jack's body tightened as he fought against having a reaction to the feeling of her soft, moist lips pressed against his. But in the end he knew it was futile and simply let himself relax and tumble headfirst into the feeling, scent and taste of her. Though the entire kiss lasted no more than ten seconds and probably seemed somewhat chaste to the curious onlookers, there was no denying that kissing Molly was an unexpectedly sensual experience, one he didn't seem to have a heck of a lot of control over.

She pulled back, smiled at him and faced their guests. "And you've brought the girls."

Witnessing her reaction, Jack didn't know whether to laugh or cry. On the one hand, she remembered her co-workers. On the other, she'd called him darling and kissed him soundly. The worst part of it was, he wasn't merely growing accustomed to having her kiss him, he was starting to enjoy it.

He cleared his throat. "Yes, Molly, I did bring your friends because—"

"Because they haven't seen the house yet," Molly interrupted him, grabbing Sophia's hands and pulling her toward the partially furnished dining room. "Don't mind the place," she said, giving the group a sideways glance as she guided everyone over the threshold. "You know how it is. Married for only six weeks, we haven't had a lot of time for decorating."

"I guess that's to be expected," Olivia said politely, but because Molly was two steps ahead of everyone and had her back to her friends, Olivia tossed Jack a completely baffled look.

He caught Olivia's arm and kept her in the foyer, as Molly began talking about "their" plans to finish "his" dining room which currently had only cherrywood furniture sitting on thick white carpeting. The room had no pictures, or flowers or finishing touches of any sort—not even a tablecloth.

"Are you understanding what I was trying to tell you?" he asked Olivia when he was sure Molly was out of hearing range.

"It's like she's the same person," Olivia said incredulously. "But she's got this whole other life dancing around in her head."

"Thank God you see it. For a minute there I was beginning to think *I* was the one who was crazy."

"Oh, you're not crazy," Rachel assured him as she, too, slipped out of the dining room. "This girl really believes what she's telling us."

"So what do I do?"

"Seems to me like you have two choices," Rachel said. "You can either sit her down and explain the truth. Or you'd better hope you've got high limits on your credit cards. Molly has a real flare for decorating, but she's also got expensive taste, and big, big ideas."

"Oh, boy," Jack said, then ran his hand down his face. "I tried this morning to explain that we weren't married, but she didn't believe me."

"Seeing us also didn't trigger her right memories," Rachel reminded him pessimistically.

"You need some kind of proof," Olivia said, thinking. "I know," she said, and snapped her fingers. "She's wearing the same clothes she had on yesterday. We all know Molly doesn't wear the same outfit twice in the same month, let alone two days back-to-back. All we have to do is show her that her clothes aren't here. That will be actual proof that she doesn't live here and maybe that will be enough of a trigger to cause her to make the connection that if she doesn't live here, you're not married."

"Hey, that's not such a bad idea," Jack said, relieved that someone had come up with at least *something* concrete. "It might actually work, if we present it to her in the right way."

"And what way is that?" Rachel asked. As she spoke, she glanced over at Molly and her expression softened. "No matter how you say it, you're going to hurt her."

Olivia shook her head. "*He's* already tried saying it. One of us will have to do the explaining this time."

"I can't!" Rachel gasped.

"Come on, Rachel. It's got to be you or me. The quickest, easiest way to do this is to question her about where her clothes are when we get to the bedroom. We don't have time to explain the plan to anyone else. One of us will have to ask her where her clothes are and the other will have to lead her into making the connection that her clothes aren't here because she doesn't live here."

Rachel drew a long breath. "All right. I'll ask where her clothes are. You lead her into realizing she doesn't live here."

"And I'll tell her we're not married," Jack piped in, once again feeling responsible and once again not willing to let someone else do his dirty work—at least not completely.

Following Rachel and Olivia, Jack slipped to the back of the line as Molly directed everyone up the steps. When they reached his bedroom and he once again noticed how sparsely furnished even that room was, the strangest—almost giddy—feeling overcame him. In the five years that he'd lived in this house, he'd come up with hundreds of reasons it was wrong to put off the decorating he'd begun with his wife. But he never worried that having a half-furnished home would aid one of his employees in believing they were married.

He shook his head in wonder. In a sense, he was getting what he deserved for dragging his feet. But every time he thought about finishing what Barbara had started, he went cold inside and couldn't do it. Now, not completing the decorating was coming back to haunt him because Molly saw this partially furnished, bare-walled house exactly for what it was. The first home of newlyweds. She saw the bed and dresser with the mismatched bedspread and curtains and she knew they hadn't been matched because there hadn't been time or money to buy the right things yet. She saw there were no pictures or embellishments because those were luxuries that came with time or treasures that came as they were discovered.

"This is a lovely, large room," Patricia said, giving Jack a look as if to tell him she didn't know what else to say or how else to react.

Before Jack could say anything, Olivia jumped in. "And that must be a great big closet back there."

"Oh, it is," Molly said, striding to the walk-in closet. She pulled open the double doors like a "Price Is Right" model revealing a new prize.

All the women peered in expectantly.

Rachel stepped forward. "Molly," she said kindly. "Honey, I don't see any of your clothes."

"No, I don't, either," Molly said, as if this were the first time the thought had struck her.

"That's odd for someone who's been married for six weeks," Olivia pointed out gently.

"Two months," Molly corrected, sounding confused.

"You told us a minute ago, you'd been married six weeks," Sophia chided, but kindly.

"I meant two months."

"Your clothes aren't here and you can't remember how

long you've been married," Olivia said, laying her arm across Molly's shoulders and directing her to sit on the bed. "Could that be because you aren't really married?"

"But I am married...."

Jack was about to jump in and as gently as possible contradict her, but she turned her tear-filled hazel eyes on him and something inside of Jack melted. Their gazes locked, and for the next several seconds, Jack couldn't think of anything but how incredibly beautiful she was and how utterly devastated she looked.

"Jack," she implored softly, "tell them that we're married. Tell them how funny our first date was when we had dinner at that restaurant and we couldn't keep our hands off each other." Without giving Jack a chance to answer, she turned to Olivia again. "Surely you remember my wedding. At the least you've got to remember my twenty-five-foot Italian lace train."

When Olivia didn't respond, she said, "There is no way you can forget a twenty-five-foot Italian lace train."

She faced Jack again. "I don't know what's going on here, but if this is a joke, I think it's very cruel."

Her tear-filled eyes held his. "Jack?"

He swallowed hard.

"Jack?"

This time after she said his name, she pressed her lips together to keep them from trembling. His heart broke, and he couldn't do what he knew he needed to do.

"That's right, darling. I'm sorry," he said, rushing to her side to comfort her. "It was a joke and a bad one. I'm sorry. You're right. We are married."

For two seconds there was nothing but complete silence, then Rachel gasped, Olivia groaned, Patricia sighed heavily, Sophia moaned and Cindy fell to the bed in complete disbelief.

"But where are my clothes?"

"Some I hid as part of the joke, and others we haven't moved from your apartment yet," Jack said, then grimaced. This was probably the stupidest thing he'd ever done in his life, but he couldn't stand to see Molly so hurt. Even going beyond his softhearted tendencies, he had to wonder if there wasn't something wrong that she was so absolutely positive they were married, and he considered that he might do her more harm than good by forcing her to see the truth.

"In fact, I'm going to go to your apartment tonight and get everything you'll need for the next couple of days," he added. "But I want you to do me a favor."

She sniffed back her tears and gave him a watery smile. "What?"

"I want you to lie down because I'm going to call a friend of mine. He's a doctor. I'm going to have him stop by just to make sure you truly weren't hurt last night when you hit your head."

"I feel fine."

"Yeah, but your memory's a little fuzzy."

"I guess," she conceded and lay down on the bed.

"Good," Jack said, and kissed her forehead, then realized that was becoming a habit.

Once he had Molly settled and everyone said their goodbyes to her, he led the women down to the foyer. "Sorry about that," he said to Olivia and Rachel. "I couldn't stand to see her so hurt."

Olivia sighed. "And you had a point about her memory. It probably wouldn't be a bad idea to have a doctor check her out."

"My best friend from grade school is a general practitioner. I'll call him from Molly's apartment and have him meet me here in about an hour."

"Would you like me to stay with her while you're gone?" Rachel asked quietly.

Jack breathed a sigh of relief. "I was hoping someone would offer."

The purse she'd left on his kitchen table contained both a driver's license with her address and keys to let him into her apartment. Twenty minutes after Molly's friends left his house, Jack was rummaging through the drawers of the dresser in Molly's bedroom. His first thought when he stepped into her small apartment was how skillfully she'd decorated the tiny space. The large, curtainless window in the back of the main room gave the place an open, airy appearance. A nubby taupe sofa sat on a black-and-gold area rug. Two black tapestry chairs bordered an oak coffee table, and the whole grouping was surrounded by plants.

Her bedroom wasn't the typical female floral fiasco. Instead, it was a blend of rich cherrywood and champagne satin with nuggets of burgundy in the burlaplike rugs and splashes in the multicolored throw pillows. The dresser and vanity were each draped with a champagne satin cloth. Pink and burgundy floral arrangements sat on both bedside tables and nothing, absolutely nothing was out of place. There wasn't even an errant sock hanging out of a drawer.

Jack couldn't help but draw the comparison of how his huge, elaborate house was unkempt and stood practically empty, while her tiny, utilitarian apartment had been made into an elegant, but comfortable, home.

After removing two pair of jeans, Jack closed the bottom drawer of her dresser. So far he'd located T-shirts, jeans and even a sweater or two, but he hadn't found any of the things she probably really needed—like clothes for work—not to mention underwear, bras and stockings.

Of course, he'd confined his search to the lower compartments, remembering that Barbara had placed her soft, intimate apparel in the smaller drawers closer to the top of the dresser.

With a sigh, Jack braved one of those smaller drawers.

Even as he opened it, pastel colors greeted him. Soft pinks. Silky blues. Sunny yellows.

He swallowed and reached inside. The shimmery fabric glided along his palm and fingertips. Without thought for color coordination or practicality, he pulled out two bras. Fringed by crisp lace, the peach bra dipped low. The black bra had no accoutrements. It didn't need them. The wicked material in and of itself would be enough to drive a sane man crazy.

Trying not to look at the underthings any more than he already had, Jack shoved those bras and several pair of underwear into the suitcase he'd found in her closet. It wasn't hard or unreasonable to imagine Molly wearing any of this. She was a soft, feminine woman. The problem was he didn't *want* to imagine Molly wearing soft, satiny things. He didn't want to imagine Molly as anything other than the intelligent, capable woman that she was.

Deciding to put himself out of his misery, Jack dumped the contents of her underwear drawer into the suitcase. He found her stocking drawer and did the same. Without any more thought or meandering, he grabbed a nightgown and robe from the back of her bathroom door, then he pulled three dresses from her closet. Since they were still on hangers, he concluded he should probably carry them rather than stuff them into the small piece of luggage.

With her clothing taken care of, Jack sat on her sofa and called Dr. Tim. Because he got Tim's answering service, Jack left his cellular number, knowing that if Tim hadn't called him by the time he got home, he would rather leave another message than risk that Tim would call his home and get Molly. Lord only knew what she'd say to him.

He gathered Molly's clothes and started back to his house. Two minutes before he would have pulled into his driveway, his cellular phone rang. "Tim?" he answered anxiously.

"Yeah, hey, how did you know it was me?"

"I didn't. I was praying it was you," Jack said, and drove his car into his driveway. "I have a very big, very odd problem."

"Well, that's refreshing," Tim said cheerfully. "It's about time you had a problem."

"Very funny," Jack said, opening the door of his Blazer and pulling out Molly's things before he started up the walk. "I didn't laugh at you when you couldn't get hotel reservations in Hawaii. No, not me. Instead, I called to our corporate liaison. I pulled some strings. I got you a room when other, probably more important doctors had to stay home from that symposium."

"All right. All right. I get the picture. I'll stop teasing. What's up?"

"One of the women who works for me, a copywriter, got a slight bump on the head last night. I swear she wasn't even knocked out, but when it was time to go home—in case she was hurt—I thought it would be better for her to spend the night at my house...."

"Yeah, right," Tim said, laughing heartily. "That's a good one. I'll have to remember that one the next time my mother calls and a woman answers."

"That's the truth."

"Really?" Tim asked, disappointed. "Lord, you're in worse shape than I thought."

"I'm fine," Jack insisted, determined to keep the conversation on track. "My copywriter isn't. I mean, she doesn't seem sick. She isn't nauseated, doesn't have a fever and isn't paralyzed or anything. But something's not right."

There was the slightest pause in conversation, long enough for Jack to recognize Tim had switched from being his overcomical best friend into being a doctor again. "What do you mean something's not right?" he asked, his tone all business now.

Jack drew a long, slow breath, not quite sure how to state

the obvious. In the end, he decided there was only one way. And that was to get right to the truth. "She thinks we're married."

Tim burst out laughing. "Jack, stop this. Your life might be boring, but I actually have a date tonight. If you only called to be stupid…"

"I didn't call to be stupid. I'm serious. The woman thinks we're married. I don't know what to do. I can't send her home like this. I'm afraid to take her to a hospital for fear that will make her worse."

"All right. All right. Hold on," Tim said. "You're only about ten minutes away from my house. I'll sweep by there on my way home from the office. I'll give you my professional opinion and I won't even charge you for the house call.… But you owe me."

"I think this makes us even for Barrington getting you the room in Honolulu," Jack said, and pushed the button that disconnected the call.

When he entered his foyer, Rachel greeted him. "She's sound asleep. Fell asleep the minute you left and hasn't woken since."

Jack blew his breath out on a long sigh. "I don't know if that's good or bad."

Rachel raised her hands helplessly. "I don't, either."

"At least Dr. Tim is on his way."

"That's a relief," Rachel said, and headed for the door. "I'd love to stay and help you, Jack, but I have plans for tonight and I can't break them."

"No, Rachel, there's no need for you to stay." Truth be known, he didn't want any more witnesses than he already had. "I'll fill you in tomorrow morning on how everything goes with Dr. Tim."

After Rachel left, Jack checked on Molly. Because she was sound asleep as Rachel had said, Jack snuck downstairs. Afraid to eat what Molly had cooked, he made himself a cup of tomato soup and a toasted cheese sandwich, and switched on his television to watch the news while he ate. Even before he was done, he heard the sound of Tim's vehicle and met him at the front door.

"How's the patient?" Tim asked as he entered. Unlike Jack, who was over six foot, Tim O'Brien was only about five foot nine and appeared to be just this side of chunky. But Tim's extra weight was mostly muscle. Because he loved rich, calorie-laden food, Tim exercised religiously. He was as solid as the Rock of Gibraltar. Wavy blond hair and mild green eyes gave him the tranquil, likeable demeanor of everybody's favorite cousin.

"Sleeping. I didn't know if that was good or bad, so I left her alone."

"That was probably for the best," Tim agreed as Jack led him upstairs and to his bedroom.

Jack stayed for the first of the examination. He watched Tim awaken Molly, watched as her eyes unerringly searched out Jack before she focused on Dr. Tim, and knew what she would tell Tim even before she said it. As Tim peered into her eyes, she confirmed that she believed she and Jack were married. While he studied the inside of her ear, she told stories of their first date. While Tim took her pulse, she gave details from their wedding. During her blood pressure reading, she explained what she planned to do with their house.

Through it all, Tim stayed straight-faced, not even showing the concern Jack felt ripping through his own nervous system. It was odd, disconcerting, to hear someone talk so seriously about things that had never happened.

When Tim explained that he'd like to listen to her heart and her breathing, and for that she'd need to unbutton her blouse, Jack left the room. He'd seen enough of her underwear for one day, but more than that, he genuinely was concerned, and he worried that he was in the way—specifically, he had a powerful urge to pace.

So he left. He made his way to his long, thin, *empty* den and paced to his heart's delight. A half hour later, Tim came jogging down the stairs.

"Jack?" he called, rounding the corner of the dining room, which Jack could see from his den.

"How is she?" Jack asked, stepping into the dining room.

"She's fine. Frankly," Tim said, grinning from ear to ear, "I'd keep her. She's cute as a bug's ear and has every intention of making you the happiest man on the face of the earth. Did you know she wants five kids?"

Jack squeezed his eyes shut. "No."

"Well, she does, and part of the reason she does is because she's sure you'll make such a good father. And I agree with her. You will make a good father. I say keep her."

Jack narrowed his eyes at Tim. "I don't find any of this in the least bit amusing. Believe it or not, I'm worried about her."

"Well, don't be," Tim said, and snapped his black bag closed. "Her parents are Dominic and Darcy Doyle. They sell self-help tapes. Part of what she remembers from yesterday is getting a package from her mother. It was a new tape on visualizing. My best guess here is that she was doing some visualizing of you as a great father, and thinking you'd be a good person to marry and have kids with, when she got knocked over and bumped her head...and somehow reality and fantasy sort of collided."

"Well if that doesn't beat all," Jack said, rolling his eyes. "I think I understand."

"Good, because she's not sick. Physically she's fine. Mentally, emotionally, she's fine. I think the combination of her visualization and waking up in your bed planted the notion in her head that you're married. But since you've tried the rational ways of getting that notion out and it didn't budge, you're going to have to wait until something equally simple shoves it out."

"You're kidding."

"Nope," Tim said, heading for the front door. "But I think I have some good news."

"I'm desperate."

"Well, I'd love to string you on into thinking you might have to live with Molly forever, but I really think all you're going to have to do is take her to work tomorrow. Ever since she hit her head, she's been in your house—unfamiliar surroundings. Let her get a good night's sleep, feed her a good breakfast and take her into familiar territory tomorrow morning and my guess is she'll be back to normal before she gets to her desk."

It made sense. It all made perfect sense. Jack breathed a sigh of relief. "Thanks, Tim. And forget what I said about the room in Hawaii. I do owe you."

"Great. I love it when people owe me. And I meant what I said. Take her to work tomorrow and she'll be fine."

Jack said goodbye and closed the door on Tim, thinking his troubles were over. But two seconds after Tim was gone, he realized he was taking Molly into a building with over a hundred people—their friends and co-workers—and if Molly didn't get her memory back, she could very well tell each and every one of them she was Jack's wife.

Chapter Four

On his way to the kitchen, Jack spotted the suitcase containing Molly's clothes. For thirty seconds, he debated leaving it downstairs and giving it to her in the morning. But he recognized that seeing her luggage or touching her things might be exactly what the doctor had ordered. If Dr. Tim was correct when he said something familiar would bring back Molly's memory, then unpacking might actually be enough to pull her into the real world again.

In fact, Jack realized, what he needed to do was have Molly unpack *right now*. Because if she got her memory back tonight, then he wouldn't have to worry about taking her to work in the morning.

Happy, almost weak with relief from his new idea, Jack grabbed the suitcase and carried it up the steps. When he reached his room, the door was closed, so he knocked twice.

Molly opened the door with a frown. "What are you doing knocking on your own bedroom door?" she playfully scolded.

"I, uh, didn't want to disturb you in case you were sleeping,'' Jack said, neatly covering his tracks as he tossed her suitcase to the bed.

"What is all this tonight? First you play that horrid practical joke,'' she reminded him, walking toward him with her fists planted on her hips. ''Now you're acting afraid to come into your own bedroom.''

When she reached him, she slipped her arms around his neck. ''If I didn't know how much you love me,'' she said, smiling up at him, her hazel eyes shining, ''I'd think we were having a marital crisis of some sort.''

As she said the last, Molly stretched to her tiptoes, and her lips began inching to his. When the sentence was complete, she chastely kissed him.

Jack decided to accept the kiss because he didn't want to jeopardize his plan, but suddenly, and without warning, the pressure of her mouth increased, her arms around his neck tightened, her body pressed against his and she was kissing him in a way that sent blistering heat the whole way to his toes.

As his completely insubordinate body dissolved into six feet, three inches of malleable flesh, Jack understood the term ''nuclear meltdown.'' *Man, but the woman could kiss*. He would have never thought that. Hell, he never would have thought any kind of sexual idea about Molly. She was... She was... She was *Molly* for Pete's sake. A decent man didn't have sexual thoughts about a co-worker. It was even more disgraceful to have sexual thoughts about an underling, a woman he supervised. It wasn't fair. It was inappropriate. It was...

Impossible to resist. Unexpectedly slammed with a particularly potent punch of desire, Jack tunneled his fingers into the hair at her nape and opened his mouth over hers. But before his fingers completely slid through her silken locks and before he'd fully tasted the sweetness of her mouth, his common sense came knocking at the back of his brain.

What the hell was he doing?

He pulled back at the same second she pulled back. But where his expression was a combination of mortification for his own moral lapse, and complete surprise that they had such explosive chemistry, Molly only smiled brightly at him.

"I'm going to put my things away."

"Good idea," Jack said, but he didn't move. Couldn't move. Surprise had him in a mortal grip. Molly was sweet. She was quiet. She was sensible. She wasn't supposed to kiss like that, but now that Jack knew that she could—and did—he also knew he'd never be able to look at her in the same way again. He wondered if he'd even be able to be in the same room with her without thinking of that wonderful, passionate, mind-numbing kiss.

Molly strode to the bed where Jack had placed her suitcase, and Jack drew a long breath. He was a professional. There was no decision to make here, no problem. He had to be able to handle being around Molly for as long as the two of them continued to work together. And, by God, he would.

"Oh," Molly said, but it came out as a shocked sigh. "What did you do? Hide *all* my lingerie at my old apartment? Good Lord, if I hadn't caught on to your little trick, I wouldn't even have been able to shower tonight! Shame on you."

"I'm sorry," Jack said, watching her eyes, hoping against hope that he'd see recognition dawn in their hazel depths, as Molly rifled through her things.

"Hey," she cried, quickly glancing over at him. "Hey, wait a minute!"

"Yes?" Jack asked expectantly.

"It just hit me," she said, gazing around his bedroom as if seeing it for the first time.

Jack held his breath.

"I didn't shower this morning. Well for heaven's sake," she said, and started unbuttoning her blouse. Making short order of her task, she easily got to the middle button, then she sighed with acceptance. "I remember now. After you sent me back to bed, I slept until about noon. When I got up I fixed myself something to eat, and when I started cleaning up after lunch, I kept cleaning. You know, things were pretty dusty around here. We're going to have to come up with a better housekeeping schedule."

By now she was at the bottom button of her blouse. Jack could see a strip of cream-colored lace peeking from behind the fawn silk.

"Yeah, I guess you're right," he said, inching toward the door. Disappointment and unwanted, unwelcome curiosity simultaneously ricocheted through him. She didn't remember anything and she wasn't going to remember anything. And if he didn't soon get out of here, she'd be completely naked because she was stripping. She honestly, genuinely thought they were married, and married people stripped—in front of each other. Without worry. Without concern. Just like she was doing now.

In spite of the fact that there was a part of him that wanted to know if she *really* wore the kind of underwear she kept in her drawers, Jack wasn't unhappy when she turned her back to him. He knew his only recourse was to retreat, but carefully, because Molly now stood between him and his destination.

Slowly, cautiously, he edged to the left, attempting to slip around her. "We probably do need a new housekeeping schedule," he said, distracting her attention from the fact that he was leaving.

"If the dust was any indicator, we don't have much choice," Molly said and, her back to him, took two steps to the left to fling her earrings to the dresser, once again placing herself directly in his path.

"Okay. You're right," Jack congenially said. Not one to be easily discouraged, he inched to his right.

But, returning to her original spot after tossing her earrings, Molly inadvertently mimicked his steps. "I didn't mind the fine powder I found in the living room, but I hate cobwebs."

Desperate, Jack quickly veered to the right. But even though she couldn't see him, Molly twisted and placed herself directly in his path.

Jack didn't know whether to laugh or cry. On the one hand, he'd gotten himself into a fairly preposterous mess, and if this had happened to any of his friends, he'd probably laugh at them. On the other hand, this was a fairly preposterous mess, and if he didn't soon get them out of it, he and Molly might do some permanent damage to their business relationship. So far, nothing actually bad had happened—unless you counted that one kiss. And Jack didn't. Yes, it was a wonderful, passionate kiss, but he was a professional and he would forget it.

As long as he could get out of this room.

As he tried to squeak past her, Molly shifted slightly to kick off her shoes and blocked his way.

"Okay, so the way we have it now, you cook and I clean up. I wash laundry and you fold...."

For a few seconds, Jack stood mesmerized, confused that her "memory" was so clear about a life they didn't have. He didn't know anything about her parents or what they taught in their self-help tapes, but they must instruct their listeners to be incredibly detailed.

"You vacuum and I dust," she continued, and reached for the button of her trousers.

Jack's eyes widened. "Molly, honey," he urged cautiously. "How about letting me get past you?"

"So, if I'm the one who dusts," she said, stepping in front of him as if she hadn't heard him, "then I'm the one who's negligent here."

As she said the last, she hooked her thumbs under the waistband of her slacks and pulled them down. Because her back was to him and because she still wore her silk blouse, all Jack really saw was her legs. But, if he hadn't known better, Jack would have thought she'd choreographed the whole scene. Slowly, methodically, she revealed inch after lovely inch of perfect thigh and calf until her trousers were a puddle on the floor and she stepped out of them.

Shaking his head, Jack said, "That's it, Molly, I have to go..." He paused when she turned and gave him a confused, wounded expression as if his harsh demeanor had injured her. "To the kitchen," he added, improvising to try and make up for his tone. Then he gripped her shoulders and shifted her enough that she wasn't blocking the door anymore. "I think something's burning."

When he reached the cool kitchen, he breathed a deep sigh of relief. Basically, that was a close one, but he'd handled it. He was out of that bedroom, and tomorrow morning when he got Molly to the office, her memory would snap back to where it was supposed to be. All he had to do was get through the night.

Get through the night? What if she expected him to sleep with her? She thought they were married! Of course she was going to expect him to sleep with her.

With a groan he sat on one of the stools at his breakfast bar and buried his face in his hands, trying to think of a way out of that, but before he got his answer, Molly snuck up on him and wrapped her arms around him.

"Sweetheart, we have to get to bed early because we both have work in the morning," she said, then began kissing his neck.

Jack's body didn't wait for instructions. Instead, it took on a life of its own, leaving his conscience behind. If he had been alone, he would have cursed it. But he wasn't alone, so he couldn't. He also knew he couldn't get out of sleeping with her—unless he wanted to hurt her. Realistically he could start an argument with her, pretend to be angry or make her angry, and then he could sleep on the couch again. Unfortunately, a picture of her sad, wounded expression sprung up before him and he knew he couldn't put her through that again. Simultaneously, however, he also realized there was no way in hell he could spend a night in the same bed with this woman—not when she thought they were married.

He turned in her arms. "Molly, are you sure it's such a good idea for us to sleep together tonight?"

She smiled at him. "What are you talking about?"

"Well, you got a pretty nasty bump on the head yesterday and Dr. Tim doesn't want you doing anything physical."

To his utter amazement, she burst into giggles. "What has gotten into you lately? You have never been shy around me before. Why can't you come right out and say we can't have sex tonight?"

He cleared his throat. Embarrassment flooded through him. He'd never spoken so brazenly to an employee before. "All right. We can't have sex tonight. Dr. Tim doesn't think it would be a good idea."

Clicking her tongue in reprimand, she bent forward, framed his face with her hands and kissed him. When she pulled back, she clicked her tongue again. "My mother always taught me that anything a married man and woman chose to do in the privacy of their own bedroom is perfectly acceptable. I hope the reason Dr. Tim put this restriction on us isn't because you explained how 'physical' we get when we get physical."

Her lips curved seductively, Molly looked him in the eye. Jack swallowed hard. *How physical we get when we get physical?* he thought, and swallowed again. If he'd wondered before about how detailed her fantasies had been, Jack knew that had been peanuts compared to how he was wondering now.

In less than twenty-four hours, Molly had taken herself

from being his nice, sweet, *safe* copywriter and had entered the world of seductress.

And he still had to get through the night with her.

Fat chance.

"Okay, Molly, since we're being up-front here, I'll admit Dr. Tim doesn't want me sleeping with you because he doesn't want me to risk bumping you and hurting you any more than you were hurt last night."

It was a lie, pure, plain and simple, but it was a lie with a purpose. She'd never forgive herself or him if she woke up with her memory tomorrow morning and found him beside her under the covers.

"So I sleep on the couch again."

Chapter Five

Jack drew a quiet, fearful breath as they pulled into the parking lot of Barrington Corporation. Molly had chattered non-stop on the way to work, but Jack hadn't focused on what she'd said. He was too darned afraid she wasn't going to get her memory back until after she'd told half the employees that they were married.

Still, he didn't have a choice but to take her inside. She needed to be around familiar people and things. And she needed to see *him* in his proper role. Dr. Tim hadn't told him that, but Jack more or less figured that out on his own. He truly believed that once Molly saw him as her real boss, not her pretend husband, all this would fall into place for her.

Like a genuine married woman, she didn't wait for him to open her car door. Instead, she jumped out and met him in front of the vehicle. They walked toward the main entrance together, smiling and waving at employees from other departments as everyone headed for various entrances to the building.

As he and Molly strode down the main corridor to the

elevator, Jack felt as if all eyes were on them. But even if people were noticing, most would only think Jack had given Molly a ride to work. A few said hello. One or two waved. A couple stopped to wait with them for the elevator.

For the most part, the only conversation was a mumbled greeting when a new person joined the waiting group. The elevator arrived. Everyone stepped in. The doors closed and the small box jerked to life.

For two floors, no one uttered a sound. They were like zombies without their morning coffee—which, Jack knew, was fairly typical—and very good news for him. But once he got over the fear that Molly was going to say something she shouldn't, or someone was going to observe something odd, Jack realized that the most important thing hadn't happened. Molly hadn't gotten her memory back. She hadn't said anything, but, then again, she didn't have to. If she were remembering, or even if her memory were merely being stimulated, her eyes would be clouded with confusion. Instead, her eyes still held that happy sparkle and her face virtually glowed.

Jack scowled. The elevator bell rang, indicating their floor, and, without thinking, he took Molly's elbow and led her into the corridor. When he recognized what he'd inadvertently done, he dropped her arm like a hot potato.

"What is wrong with you this morning?" Molly whispered.

Glad for her discretion, though somewhat confused by it, Jack glanced at her. "I'm just tired."

"No one told you to sleep on the couch," Molly reminded him quietly.

"I believe Dr. Tim told me."

"Well, I'll make it up to you tonight," Molly said, then raised herself to her tiptoes and kissed his cheek before she pivoted and walked into her office.

Jack felt his face turn fire-engine red. Mortified, he quickly

looked around, but the only person who appeared to have seen
was Sandy Johnson, the department secretary.

"She was thanking me for the ride into work," Jack said,
then strode toward his office, not about to let the blue-eyed,
brown-haired romantic draw her own conclusions. "I don't
want any calls this morning. Not one," he added as he walked
through the door, which he slammed. He didn't know why
he was so irritable. Truthfully, he didn't care if the other
employees gossiped about him. And he *did* want Molly to get
her memory back, so she needed to be here to get stimulated.
So why the hell did he feel that leaving Molly alone in her
office was the biggest mistake of his life?

Because it was! Jack realized, all his nerve endings jumping. He stashed his briefcase in his closet and ran to the door
again. He might want her to get her memory back, but that
didn't mean he was abandoning all this to chance. At the very
least, he was doing some damage control.

After ripping open his office door, Jack dashed down the
hall again, but when he reached Molly's office, he was surprised to find that she had her door closed. Through the glass
pane of the top half of the door, he could see Molly working
diligently, her head bent low as she tallied figures.

Like a parent peeking in on his newborn child and discovering she was content, Jack breathed a sigh of relief and tip-
toed away, back to his own office.

When he passed her, Sandy raised an eyebrow in question.
He smiled at her. "Molly's feeling a little under the
weather. I was checking on her."

Sandy smiled, but she gave Jack a look as if to say she
didn't believe him. Jack merely stepped into his office, closing the dark wood double doors behind him.

He was far, far too old for this.

"So how do you feel?"

Molly glanced up from her computer screen. "I feel fine,"

she said, sounding confused. "And I think it's time you and everyone else stopped asking me. I'm starting to think Dr. Tim told you I was going to die in two days or something. He didn't tell you that, did he?"

"No, no," Jack said, leaning his hip on her desk, getting comfortable. "Really, he said you're terrific. He also said the day at work would be good for you. Did you have a good day?" he asked, knowing that each and every one of her friends had been up to call on her to try to prod her memory as he had instructed them.

"Jack, the day is only half over."

"I know that, but I'm just checking to see if you're...you know, finding anything that helps you...." *Remember we're not married.* He almost said it. He'd spent the entire morning alternately pacing his office and peeking toward hers, but Molly had closed her door, parked herself on her chair and hadn't moved all morning. Except for the visitors he'd sent in to attempt to nudge her memory, no one had bothered her.

For every bit as much as he'd prayed someone unusual would pop in on her and say something that would make her remember her real life, he also prayed no one would visit her so she couldn't tell yet another person she believed them to be married and drag yet another innocent bystander into this charade.

"Helps me what?" Molly asked, staring at him. "Helps me plow through these demographics any more quickly? Frankly, no. Jack, I've told you a hundred times I don't like to rush these. This is one area I excel at so I think we're better off to take my opinion than yours—even though you are the boss."

"You're right," Jack said, discouraged because she'd dashed one of his big hopes. Basically she told him that she knew he was her boss, but that hadn't jarred her memory. The drive to work hadn't jarred her memory. Her office hadn't jarred her memory. Seeing her co-workers hadn't jarred her memory. And now obviously seeing their respective roles at the office hadn't jarred her memory.

As far as he was concerned, this experiment had failed.

"Then what are you driving at?" she asked, but a sort of understanding dawned. He could see it in her facial expression. "Oh, I remember. It's my turn to buy lunch," she said, rising from her seat and grabbing her purse. "I forgot we had that little tradition where I buy lunch every other day. Since you bought on Wednesday and I wasn't here Thursday, that makes today my turn. Okay, let's go."

The fact that she had such vivid, detailed recollections of things they always "did" confused Jack so much, his brow furrowed. He didn't picture Molly to be much of a daydreamer, but then again he hadn't thought she'd be such a terrific kisser, either. If Molly was surprising him, Jack decided she was doing it in spades. He couldn't believe he'd paid so little attention to her that he really didn't know her at all.

Though it was only a quarter till twelve, Jack realized that leaving wasn't such a bad idea. Bringing her here hadn't exactly been a mistake. It was an experiment that had to be tried, but it hadn't worked. Now he had to get Molly out of here before she said something to somebody. Cutting out early for lunch was only the beginning.

Caught up in praying Molly stayed quiet, Jack didn't give any consideration to whether or not anyone noticed them departing together. He pushed the down button on the elevator, and stood beside Molly who was unexpectedly demure. Given this moment of peace and tranquillity to reflect, Jack concluded that though Molly hadn't regained her memory, he could at least be thankful that she hadn't embarrassed them, either.

Even as he thought the last, Jack shifted to the right and saw Mr. Barrington striding toward them. Mercifully, the elevator bell rang and the doors whooshed open. Jack shoved

Molly into the elevator and jumped in after her, but his sigh of relief was cut off when Rex Barrington called, "Hold that for me, would you, Jack?"

Damn! Jack's finger teetered above the Close Door button, but in the end his common sense won. Molly hadn't embarrassed him up to now. She appeared to be preoccupied with work. And it truly was bad form to ignore a request from the man who paid your salary. Slowly, but resignedly, Jack's finger moved to the Open Door button. He held it in until Mr. Barrington had entered, then he released it and the door whooshed closed.

"So, congratulations on that layout the other day," Rex Barrington said, glancing from Molly to Jack. His conventional black suit was stiff and formal and he wore his gray hair in a no-nonsense traditional style. But his green eyes sparkled with fatherly warmth. "Just got there under the wire, I hear."

"Yes, we did," Jack said, characteristically proud of his department. "I have a great team."

"You certainly do."

"Jack's very loyal to his staff," Molly put in with a laugh. "Always giving them the credit when he deserves most of it."

"That's about fifty percent true, Molly," Mr. Barrington corrected good-naturedly. "A department head is only as good as the staff he supervises. Besides, one of the people to whom Jack typically gives most of the credit is you."

Molly laughed again. "Is that so?" she asked, and the conversation was so normal, so much like any other conversation they'd held in the past that Jack didn't even feel the other shoe falling until it landed on his head, when Molly said, "I suppose it's to be expected that a man would say good things about his..."

Knowing that Molly was about to say "wife," Jack almost panicked and pasted his hand across her mouth, but he didn't.

Instead, he quickly interrupted, saying, "*Right-hand person.* It's to be expected that a man would say good things about his right-hand person. And Molly is certainly that," Jack continued, knowing he was now babbling, but he was not about to give Molly another chance to talk. At least not to Mr. Barrington. It was one thing to hope speaking with her peers would jog her memory. It was quite another to let her chatter with the company president.

Luckily the elevator reached the ground floor. When the doors opened, Mr. Barrington motioned for Molly to exit before him and she smiled graciously at him. "You know," she said, glancing back at Mr. Barrington. "We've never had you over for dinner."

"No," Mr. Barrington said, confused. "You haven't."

Again not giving himself time to panic, Jack took Molly by the shoulders and turned her to the right. "Molly, there's the first-floor ladies' room. You probably want to powder your nose before we leave for the restaurant."

As if obeying him were second nature, Molly nodded. "Okay. Be back in a minute. And I mean that about dinner, Mr. Barrington. I'll arrange something with your secretary."

The second he was sure Molly couldn't hear him, Jack pivoted to face Rex Barrington. "Our department goes out to dinner about once a month, or we have nights out like we had this Wednesday," he explained quickly. "To celebrate our success, everyone from the department went to Mahoney's. I bought a few pizzas and a couple pitchers of beer and we kicked back a bit."

"Ah, now it's starting to fall into place for me," Mr. Barrington said slyly. "Now I understand why you have the most dependable employees in the company, and why they work so hard for you. I'd like to see one of these gatherings."

"And like Molly said, we'd love to have you."

"Okay," Mr. Barrington said, then glanced at his watch as if checking if the conversation with Jack had made him late.

"I sincerely do want Molly to let my secretary know the next time your department's planning something. I'll be there."

Jack smiled and nodded, watching the whole time as Mr. Barrington exited the building and walked to where his Mercedes waited immediately beyond the doors. Once the car began pulling away, he collapsed against the wall.

"I think you should take another afternoon off."

Molly's gaze swung up from her chef's salad. "I told you I'm two weeks behind with those demographics."

"But you're looking a little pale," Jack argued carefully. "Remember. Dr. Tim said you can't overdo it."

"Lord, you'd think I was pregnant or something."

Jack's eyes widened with horror. That was a rumor he wouldn't so easily squelch. "You're not, are you?"

"No, silly," she said, laughing. "You'd be the first person to know if I was."

Jack gave himself a moment to let his pulse and blood pressure lower. As interesting as her imagination was, it wouldn't have surprised him if she'd conjured a pregnancy, a few kids or even a dog. Thank God, she hadn't. When he was calm again, he was more convinced than ever that he needed to keep her out of the office until she got her memory back—her real memory.

"You know," he said, pretending preoccupation with his salad so she wouldn't guess that he was trying to manipulate her. "Having our friends over the other night caused me to think that it really is time to get a few new things for the house."

Molly smiled at him. "We have plenty of time. I'm sure our friends understand that we can't decorate a whole house in six weeks."

"No, but it would have been nice to have decent curtains in the living room."

"You mean window treatments," Molly said, her eyes shining with anticipation.

"Is that the same thing as curtains?"

"A little fancier," Molly said, then she grimaced. "And probably a little more expensive."

"Molly, we don't have to worry about money," Jack said, but he caught his slip, and realized that he'd been playing along so well and for so long that he was falling into this role as if he were made for it. He shook his head as if to bring himself back to reality, but to Molly he said, "Take some time, measure the windows, figure out what matches the carpeting, do whatever it is people do to make their windows beautiful, then go buy what you need."

"Oh, that sounds great but I have that—"

"Whatever it is, it can wait," Jack said urgently. He saw Sophia walking to the cashier to pay her lunch bill, and even as he did he was struck with the idea that he didn't want Molly out in the city by herself. "Could you excuse me for a minute?"

"Sure," Molly said absently and focused on her salad again.

"Sophia," Jack called, trying to get her attention before she left the cashier.

She turned and smiled at him. "Hey, Jack. What are you doing here?"

"Molly and I are having lunch."

Sophia leaned around Jack to get a peek at Molly, and she winced. "Still thinks you're married, doesn't she?"

"And planning a family."

"Yikes."

"We had a close call with Mr. Barrington this morning. I can't take her back," Jack explained, hoping against hope Sophia could help him. "I told her she could buy new drapes for our—my—living room. She actually seems to want to do that more than study her new demographics." He paused, drew in a short breath. "But I can't let her go alone...."

"Give me your credit card and say no more," Sophia said, holding her palm up. "But you have to explain to the people in personnel why I'm taking the afternoon off."

"I'll tell them I sent you on a special Barrington project," Jack said and handed her his credit card.

Sophia glanced down at the shiny platinum card. "What's the credit limit on this?"

"Higher than your yearly salary."

"I think Molly and I are going to have a wonderful afternoon."

Jack didn't have any doubt about that, but a few minutes later as he watched Sophia escort Molly out of the restaurant while he paid their lunch bill, he privately acknowledged that losing a few hundred dollars to drapes didn't bother him. He now had an entire afternoon in which to get some work done. He didn't have to worry about what Molly would say and to whom she'd say it. And tomorrow was Saturday, so he didn't have to make up an excuse for why he couldn't take Molly to work. They could spend the whole day at home without him having to answer one question as to why.

Smiling, he stepped out into the warmth of early-afternoon sunshine, but as quickly as his smile appeared, it faded. Tomorrow *was* Saturday. And they *could* spend the whole day at home. They could spend the *whole weekend* at home.

Two long, quiet, intimate days with a woman who thought they were married and kissed him as if they'd been lovers for years.

He wasn't going to survive this.

Chapter Six

Jack knew that Molly would probably be able to laugh about this whole mess when she got her memory back, as long as nothing "happened" between them. So to get out of being in the same bed with her that night, he once again used the excuse that Dr. Tim didn't want them sleeping together.

But that reasoning brought out yet another dimension to this problem. As he lay awake on his old, worn-out sofa Friday night, Jack suddenly realized that the longer this went on, the greater likelihood that Molly would be embarrassed unless he kept things as simple as possible.

Preoccupied as he was with worry over Molly, Jack didn't fall asleep until after two, and he wasn't surprised that she woke before him on Saturday morning. Unfortunately, because he was asleep and not prepared for the assault on his senses, he again jumped with alarm at the unexpected kisses on the back of his neck. And again, before he thought about what he was doing, he sprang over the back of the couch to get out of her reach.

"Jack, what is wrong with you?" she asked dejectedly.

"I...uh...I was...having a nightmare," he said, relieved when he came up with something that would appease her without hurting her feelings. He'd never been in such a quandary before. This was not the kind of predicament safe, comfortable, harmless Jack Cavanaugh got himself into. This was the kind of messy dilemma Dr. Tim landed in.

"Well, come here," she soothed. "I'll help you forget about it."

He wasn't even going to risk asking how she planned to help him forget about it. Instead, having been awake long enough to get his brain working, he quickly changed the subject. "Actually, Mol," he said, not even noticing he'd given her a nickname. "Lying on that lumpy sofa last night, I decided that since you've chosen drapes..."

"Window treatments," Molly happily corrected.

"Window treatments," he conceded with a nod, "for this room, it would probably also be a good idea to get some new furniture. Maybe even something nice like that tapestry stuff you have in your living room."

As if considering his suggestion, Molly pursed her lips and glanced around, but as she did, her eyes began to glaze over. Jack could only guess that while trying to draw on the memory of the living room furniture in her apartment she had hooked into reality and it was holding on to her. She looked as if she were halfway between here and the truth, and the truth was winning. Any second now, he expected her to tumble into the real world again.

Waiting, hoping, Jack stood frozen, but she blinked, once, very, very slowly, and when she opened her eyes, all the confusion was gone. However, she put her hand to her forehead as if she were dizzy and said, "Yes, you're right."

Deflated, almost annoyed, Jack's shoulders hunched. He had seen—physically seen—that she was a gnat's eyelash away from returning to the real world, and he mentally cursed himself because they were at *his* house instead of *her* apartment. From that ten-second episode, Jack knew with absolute certainty that if she'd been in familiar surroundings, she would have snapped back. Being so preoccupied with keeping her out of harm's way, he'd forgotten that the office wasn't the only familiar surrounding in her life. Jack could use her apartment and her car to try to bring Molly back from her dreamworld.

"We're going to your apartment," he announced without preamble or explanation.

"Now?" Molly asked, gaping at him as if he were crazy.

"Right now," Jack said, seeing from her glowing cheeks and clean clothes that she'd been up long enough to have showered and dressed. "If you want some breakfast, grab it while I shower."

He started out of the room, but Molly caught his arm. "Why are we going to my apartment?"

"For decorating ideas," Jack said, and almost laughed. The truth of the matter was he probably could get decorating ideas from her apartment, but to bring his story in line with an explanation she could understand, he added, "We'll see what you have and make a list so we don't end up buying something we don't need."

If you can't convince them, confuse them, Jack thought as he jogged up the steps, leaving Molly standing in the living room puzzling over that. This new course of action gave him a burst of energy and he showered and dressed quickly, not wanting to lose his momentum—or hers.

In the car he said, "You remember that you fell Wednesday night?"

She nodded.

"Well, we had been at Mahoney's because our entire department was celebrating getting an advertising layout in on time."

She nodded again.

So far so good.

"Because you hit your head when you fell, I wouldn't let you drive, which means your car is still at Mahoney's. So we're going to go to Mahoney's now to get it."

"Okay."

"You do feel up to driving, don't you?"

"Yes, Jack," she said, laughing. "I'm fine. I'm sure even Dr. Tim would say I was fine. It's sweet that you're taking such good care of me. But it's not necessary."

Because it was Saturday morning, there were no cars parked around Molly's Lexus. It sat alone, deserted, in the parking lot for the restaurant/bar.

"There it is," Jack announced, and held his breath, waiting for her reaction.

For a few seconds she stared at her car, then, sighing heavily, she faced him. "This was poor planning on our part. We should have picked up my car on the way home."

Having parked his Blazer, Jack slumped over the steering wheel. "Why?"

"Because now we'll have to take two vehicles shopping."

He stared at her. It seemed impossible that she could think through the more complex issues of their problem, yet normal, average things eluded her.

"We'll leave your car at your apartment," he said, satisfied that he'd found a way to stay one step ahead of her.

"Okay," she said blithely, brushed a kiss across his cheek and jumped out of his Blazer.

Jack watched in amazement as she retrieved her keys from her purse, pressed the button to deactivate her car alarm and hopped inside her Lexus as if nothing were amiss. Confused, but still far too concerned with Molly's welfare to push things too far, he opened his window and said, "Follow me to your apartment."

She nodded happily.

Jack drove out onto the street again and hoped he genuinely would lead her home as he guided her to her real residence.

Using her key, he let her into her apartment and waited expectantly beside the front door. But she merely breezed by her nubby taupe sofa and black tapestry chairs as if they were nothing special. Then he looked on in amazement as she gathered more clothes from her bedroom, rubbing her face against soft sweaters as if they were long-lost friends, but seemingly not having any concrete understanding of why she'd missed them.

The brain, he concluded, was an unbelievable mystery. Molly remembered where her clothes were, she remembered to find a pencil to create their furniture shopping list, but she hadn't yet figured out that they weren't truly married.

"Okay, that's it," she said, stashing her notebook in her purse. "Most of this stuff isn't going to fit the decor of the house," she said, indicating her own furniture, and Jack was eternally grateful for that. When she finally snapped back into reality again, he'd hate to have her living room set in his home. "So we're going to have to start from scratch."

"I don't mind," Jack said, initially to placate her, but he realized that he literally didn't mind. First, his house did need to be decorated. Second, Molly had the good taste and decorating sense to do it. Third, he suddenly understood that all he had to do when Molly regained her memory was explain that they'd spent their time furnishing his empty house. Not only would she know she hadn't done anything stupid, but she'd see she'd spent her time productively and even helped him.

If that didn't ease her conscience and soothe her ego, nothing would.

"It's too purple."

"No, it's not. This couch is wine. And it would contrast nicely with the white carpeting and next to the cherrywood furniture of the dining room."

Jack eyed the one-color, nonskid leather sofa skeptically.

He had to admit he liked it. He *really* liked it. But they'd already purchased a homey, overstuffed floral grouping for his family room, complete with end tables with ceramic tile tops to lessen—if not completely eliminate—damage from eating while viewing TV. They'd bought lamps, chosen area rugs and picked out pictures. In a matter of four hours Molly had made the purchases that would transform his nondescript house into a home. If they didn't soon stop, Jack wouldn't be able to go into one room of his house without thinking of Molly.

"Hey, Jack, look. I'm Cleopatra."

At Molly's request, Jack turned to his right and saw that while he had been pondering, Molly had stretched out on a backless black fake fur sofa and was dangling a bunch of wax grapes above her mouth.

"Get off there," he said, glancing around quickly to see if anyone was watching. When he realized there wasn't another soul in sight, he shook his head. "You are really silly."

"Of course, I am," she agreed good-naturedly, and bounced from the sofa. Happily and completely without reserve, she brushed a soft kiss across his mouth. "That's why you married me. I balance out your stuffiness."

"I'm not stuffy," he protested. As her arms went around his neck, he noticed how naturally and easily his hands drifted to the swell of her hips. He knew a stuffy person wouldn't be so bold, then also recognized *he* wouldn't be so bold if it weren't for the fact that she genuinely believed they were married. "Am I stuffy?"

With an expression of mock distress, she nodded solemnly. "Oh, everybody thinks you're fun-loving and wonderful, but I see something no one else sees. You take your duties seriously. You pamper your employees. If you could, I think you'd bear the weight of the world on your shoulders, if only because you don't want anyone else to have to do it. You're unselfish, Jack Cavanaugh."

"I'm not unselfish," he said, and reluctantly took his hands from her hips and placed them on her wrists so he could remove her arms from around his neck. "I'm doing what I need to do to get everything done."

"That's exactly what you want everybody to believe. That you're a carefree guy who has all the time in the world to slather his employees with attention and good deeds—all so they'll be more productive. But I know the truth."

Because she walked away without pushing the issue, Jack got the distinct impression that she did know the truth. But she couldn't.

No one did.

At least not completely.

"Well, Mrs. I-Know-the-Truth," Jack said, gripping her elbow to keep her from wandering too far, "you win. We'll get the couch."

"Really!" Her eyes lit with joy, and something like a punch hit Jack in the stomach. Pleasing someone had never been so easy, or so much fun. Molly wasn't childlike in her appreciation. That would have been easy to handle. No, Molly was very adult in her gratitude—which made it all the more perilous to his ego because he knew it meant something. Without even taking a breath, he felt his chest swell a good two inches.

"I'll go get the clerk," she volunteered enthusiastically.

Jack studied her as she walked away—the confident set of her back, the swing of her derriere, the long smooth length of leg—and he wondered if he'd had his head in a basket for the past four years. All this time, he'd been working with a gorgeous blonde, with a wonderful sense of humor, and a sixth sense about him that seemed to be right on the money. And he hadn't noticed.

When she returned with the clerk, Molly continued to be bubbly with joy. So much so, that, as the young man wrote out the slip for their sofa, she easily twisted around and placed a happy kiss on Jack's lips. Without thinking, Jack put both his hands on her shoulders to keep her from quickly twisting away again. He gazed into her sparkling hazel eyes and saw things he didn't think he'd ever see again. Happiness. Enthusiasm. Hope. Tomorrow.

He actually saw tomorrow.

With the promise of tomorrow hovering in his subconscious, Jack bent his head and kissed Molly. It wasn't a pretend kiss to keep her content and semiquiet. This time when he pressed his lips to hers, it was a conscious decision. It was an expression of emotion. It was a welcome home to joy.

Molly turned the rest of the way in his arms and looped her arms around his neck. As his lips toyed with hers, Jack allowed his hands to slide down her back and then up again, feeling the reality of her, a dam of emotion welling up inside him.

Molly pulled away. "Jack, I think the clerk wants you to sign the slip for the credit card."

Mystified, mesmerized, Jack only stared at her.

"Mrs. Cavanaugh," the clerk said, then nervously cleared his throat. "You could sign."

But she couldn't, Jack realized suddenly. She couldn't sign anything "Molly Cavanaugh."

"I'll do that," Jack said, and snatched the credit card slip before the clerk could hand it to Molly. They weren't really married and she wasn't fully aware of what they were doing. Oh, she might understand purchasing furniture, but she didn't have a clue of what was happening with their kisses.

Even *he* didn't understand what was happening with their kisses. But he did know one thing. Acting on his attraction to her was about the stupidest thing he could do right now. Second only to imagining that he might have even deeper, stronger feelings than attraction.

When the clerk left, it was Jack who nervously cleared his throat. "I guess it's time to go."

Not noticing anything was wrong, Molly took his hand. "Are you trying to tell me we've exhausted the limit on your credit card?"

Jack laughed. Leave it to her to make him laugh. Again. *How had he missed this for so many years?*

"We haven't exhausted the limits on my cards. But we will be getting one hell of a delivery next Thursday. In fact," Jack said and glanced at his watch. "I should…"

"Molly? Molly is that you?"

Jack looked up in time to see a very stylish older couple almost running up the aisle to meet them.

"April? Don?" Molly said, sounding as confused as the pair who were striding toward her.

"Well, for Pete's sake," Don said, clutching Molly and enveloping her in a bear hug. "What the heck are you doing here?"

"Jack and I are getting some new furniture," Molly said as the big man released her. "What are you guys doing here?"

"We're decorating our den," the woman, April, said, as she eyed Jack critically. "Who is this?"

"Oh, oh," Molly said as if they'd caught her off guard. "This is Jack. Jack, these are my parents' oldest and dearest friends, April and Don Jenkins."

As he shook hands with Don Jenkins, Jack felt little beads of perspiration forming on his upper lip. He wasn't sure why he was worried. Molly had only introduced him as "Jack." She'd offered no further explanation. Still, the calculating expression in April's pale blue eyes clearly told Jack that this woman was scouring for more.

As if on cue, April said, "And Jack is…"

"Her boss…"

"My husband…"

April's eyebrows shot skyward. Good old Don looked as if he'd swallowed something that didn't agree with him.

"You're *married?*" April managed in an incredulous voice.

"Six weeks," Molly proudly reported.

"You ran away," April reasoned dejectedly.

Molly shook her head. "No, we had the biggest wedding this side of the Mississippi."

At first, April only stared at Molly, then she said, "Oh," her voice small and confused. "Congratulations."

Jack had never felt so miserable in his life. He knew why this conversation was flying over Molly's head. If she'd imagined they had a big wedding, in her mind her parents' best friends would have been at that wedding—or at least they would have been invited. In reality, neither had happened.

Don recovered first. "Come on, April, we'd better get shopping or it will be next August before we get that den finished." He took April's arm and moved her in the direction of bookcases and entertainment units. Politely, but distantly, he nodded to Jack. "It was a pleasure to meet you."

"The pleasure was mine," Jack said quietly, and watched them walk away. There wasn't anything he could do right this second, but after he engaged Molly in another shopping project and after enough time had passed that she wouldn't be suspicious, he would have to find the Jenkinses and come up with some sort of reasonable story.

"You know what?" he said, pulling away after the Jenkinses' departure. "I think you should pick out a bedroom set before we leave."

Molly gasped in alarm. "Absolutely, no!"

"Why not? We have three empty bedrooms. We'll make one of them into a guest room."

Molly sighed heavily, and when she faced him, Jack could see the lines of exhaustion etched in her face and knew what she was going to say even before she said it. "We might have three empty bedrooms, but if we don't soon leave, I'll drop where I stand."

"Are you sick?" Jack asked, and hastily seized her arm.

"No, just dizzy—tired."

For some odd reason, Jack didn't believe her. Maybe his own sixth sense was beginning to kick in. Or maybe he knew that because Molly wasn't the complaining kind, she wouldn't tell him when she was feeling sick or in pain, she'd simply snatch the easy excuse—being tired—and run with it. "I'm calling Dr. Tim when we get to the house."

Molly smiled wickedly and began to walk away. "Good, then I'll ask him when we can sleep together again."

Jack scrambled after her. "Is that blackmail?"

"No. But it is a logical question. If you call the doctor, I'm asking the obvious."

Chapter Seven

"**I** want you to consider it a personal favor."

Dr. Tim grinned. His green eyes danced with devilment. "Let's see," he said, holding out his hands as if they were scales. "Grant you a personal favor which makes me feel reasonably benevolent." He indicated his right hand as if placing that statement in its palm, then he nodded to his left hand. "Or use my power and authority to have one hell of a good laugh at your expense by telling your lovely wife there is no more reason the two of you can't sleep together."

Tim alternately raised and lowered each hand as if weighing the decision. "Gee, Jack, there's not much of a dilemma here."

"I'm going to give you a dilemma," Jack said, his temper snapping. "That woman in there is *not* my wife," he said, thrusting his thumb in the direction of the master bedroom. "When she gets her memory back and realizes that, she's going to be horribly embarrassed. You've had many a good laugh at my personal expense. And I'm going to admit I've had many a good laugh at yours. But this time it's not merely me you're potentially hurting. Molly's a nice girl, a sweet girl. It will downright humiliate her if we don't keep this situation in line."

Tim immediately sobered. "I'm sorry. You're right. I know you're right. It's just that it's been so long—five years—" he clarified carefully, obviously gauging Jack's reaction before he continued, "since you've been a part of the human race. I know what you've been doing. Trying to keep your life uncomplicated and perfect so you don't get hurt again, but Jack..."

Jack stopped him with one raised finger. "Don't play therapist. I'm fine. I've always been fine. And you're not here to see me, you're here to see Molly. She had a dizzy spell at the furniture store. To be perfectly honest with you," Jack said, pulling Tim a little farther down the upstairs hall and away from the bedroom door, "I think she was on the verge of getting her memory back."

It had taken him until they pulled into the driveway before Jack realized that seeing her parents' friends had jolted her memory and maybe even made her anxious, which was why she'd become pale. She hadn't been sick. She hadn't been in pain. She'd been so confused, it had weakened her.

"We'd run into friends of her parents after we signed the papers to buy a new sofa, and as they were walking away she got dizzy."

"So what makes you think she was getting her memory back?"

"It happened once before," Jack admitted with a sigh. "This morning. I mentioned wanting to furnish my living room similar to *her* living room. She started to consider it and her eyes glazed over. Then she glanced around as if she were totally confused. But rather than get her memory back, she got dizzy."

"Almost as if getting dizzy was the result of stopping her memory," Dr. Tim speculated quietly.

Jack reluctantly agreed. "Almost. I couldn't say for sure."

"Well, I couldn't say for sure, either. I'm not a psychiatrist. I'm not even a neurologist. I'm just a simple country doctor."

"I don't think she needs a psychiatrist or a neurologist. Right at this minute, I think she needs someone to confirm that her dizzy spell wasn't from something other than confusion."

"Jack, I don't know," Tim said, and caught Jack's hand before he opened the bedroom door. "This falls so much out of my area of expertise that I'm getting uncomfortable. I know it's only been three days, but if she doesn't have her memory back by tomorrow afternoon I want you to let me make an appointment for her with a friend of mine—a specialist."

Jack drew a long, resigned breath. "Yeah, I guess you're right."

"Of course I'm right," Tim cockily said, then pushed open the bedroom door.

With the covers primly folded over her lap, Molly sat braced against the headboard of Jack's bed, wearing high-collared red satin pajamas. The minute she saw Jack behind Dr. Tim she smiled and held out her hand. "See, a little nap and I'm fine. I told you this was nothing to worry about."

Jack automatically took the hand Molly extended and sat on the bed beside her, but Dr. Tim opened his black bag. "So, Jack tells me you've had these dizzy spells before," Dr. Tim prodded casually.

She nodded. "Yes."

Tim put the blood pressure cuff on her arm and pulled out his stethoscope. "They don't seem to scare you."

Molly shrugged. "They go away on their own. As quickly as they come, they're gone. I don't even have to sit down. All I have to do is focus on what I'm doing and they go. And once they're gone, I'm not dizzy anymore."

"What do you mean when you say focus on what you're

doing?'' Dr. Tim persisted, attending to the blood pressure gauge.

Molly pursed her lips. "I know this is going to sound weird, but I sort of have to remind myself of who I am, where I am and what I'm doing."

Tim peeked at Jack, then back at Molly. "And how often has this happened?"

She shrugged. "A few times, maybe four."

Tim snapped his bag closed. "Okay. I've heard enough," he said, and rose from her bed. "Molly, physically you're fine. But though I'm not a neurologist, the fact that you have to remind yourself of who you are makes me think there's a little more to this than meets the eye. So, Monday morning I'm going to make an appointment for you with a friend of mine."

She looked at Jack. "Another doctor?"

"A specialist," Jack said gently, not wanting to use the word psychiatrist, though he had a sneaky feeling that's the kind of specialist to which Tim was referring. "You did hit your head...."

"And you think there's something wrong?" Molly questioned fearfully, holding his gaze.

It was on the tip of Jack's tongue to tell her the truth, that she had only a selective memory and currently they were living a lie. But in her fragile condition, he didn't think that was the best thing to do. At the same time, he no longer felt comfortable withholding the whole truth from her, either. Particularly since it almost appeared she had a hand in keeping herself in this delusional state.

"I don't think there's anything *wrong* with you," he said, trying to reassure her. "But, like Dr. Tim, I also think it's odd that you have to remind yourself of who you are."

"Regardless of what happens, Molly, I'll be by on Monday night," Tim said. He squeezed her free hand once, then headed for the door.

Jack pressed a kiss to her forehead, and rose from his bed. "I'm going to see Dr. Tim out. Why don't you try to go back to sleep?"

Still preoccupied with Dr. Tim's suggestion, Molly nodded absently.

Jack met Tim in the downstairs foyer.

"It's obvious to me," Tim said as he snagged the front door handle, "that she doesn't want to remember who she is. It could be because she doesn't like who she is, or it could be—like her friends told you—*this* is who she *wants* to be."

Jack raked his fingers through his hair. Tim's assessment didn't fill him with annoyance at the inconvenience to his life; he was more upset about Molly. Though he'd always been concerned about Molly, there was a new dimension, a new level of anxiety that he didn't quite understand. "I don't know what to think."

"Well, if you want my opinion, because there is nothing physically wrong with her, and because she's all but admitted she's pushing back her real memories, I think we could force her into remembering who she is—" Tim began, but Jack interrupted him.

"Absolutely not."

"I know. You tried this once before and you couldn't handle it. But think about this, Jack," Tim warned. "How is *she* going to handle it when she realizes you played along when you could have forced her back into reality?"

"I don't know," Jack said, and shoved his wayward hair off his forehead. "I just know I don't want to force her into anything. There's a reason she refuses to get her memory back. I can feel it."

"I'd have to say she likes being your wife," Tim speculated knowingly. "Her parents are multimillionaires. She has a good job. She has plenty of friends. You yourself said she has a beautiful apartment. She has everything a woman could want...."

"Except a husband?" Jack suggested carefully, feeling that analysis was way off base. "That's far too simple, far too shallow a motive for Molly."

"Don't be so modest. You're quite a catch, Jack," Tim said, then pinched his cheek. "I'll call you tomorrow."

Jack waited for Tim to leave, then went into the kitchen to scrounge for supper. Despite the fact that they'd had a big lunch, Jack decided he'd fix something nice for dinner then take Molly a tray in an attempt to cheer her up. Unfortunately, when he opened the refrigerator door, he didn't even find enough eggs to make a decent omelet.

"What are you doing?"

Jack jumped at the sound of Molly's voice and bumped his head as he pulled himself out of his refrigerator. "Ouch! Molly, what are you doing up?"

"I'm hungry."

He eyed her skeptically. "Are you sure you're well enough to be out of bed?"

"I'm fine," she emphatically stated. "I think you and Dr. Tim are a little on the crazy side because you keep insisting there's something wrong with me, but I'm fine."

Jack avoided the touchy issue by giving her the bona fide bad news. "We don't have anything to make for dinner."

Her brow furrowed. "Are you sure?"

Jack took another peek into his refrigerator. "There's lots of stuff in here, but none of it falls together to be a dinner I can make."

Molly said, "Hmm," and walked to the refrigerator. "How hungry are you?"

"Fairly hungry, but not starved."

"Can you make due with French toast?"

He thought about that. He hadn't had French toast in years. And he'd loved French toast. "French toast would be great."

"Good. You set the table and I'll make the French toast."

They worked together in companionable silence for the

time it took for Molly to create their dinner and Jack to pre-
pare the table. When they sat down to eat, however, the silence wasn't relaxed anymore. Jack knew that the longer he
let it rein, the greater the possibility that Molly would begin
worrying about her upcoming doctor visit. And he didn't want
that to happen.

He cleared his throat. "This is very good."

"It's one of my specialties," she admitted around a laugh.

Surprised by her laughter, he stared at her. "You sound
like you think there's something wrong with being able to
make French toast."

"No," she said, shaking her head. "I'm laughing because
that's about as far as my specialties go."

"No, it isn't," Jack contradicted playfully, thinking this
was a terrific way to get her mind off her troubles—maybe
even the troubles she kept pushing away. "You have lots of
great things going for you."

"Really? Like what?"

He thought about telling her that she was so good at her
job that he was on the verge of offering her the position as
his assistant, which would eventually lead into overseeing a
section of his department that he felt could splinter off. But
he realized that was a discussion better left for when she was
back to normal. "You're intelligent and organized and very,
very thorough," he said, hitting the essence of what he
wanted to say without coming right out and telling her about
the promotion. "You're probably the most efficient person in
my department."

Molly frowned. "Whatever happened to 'Molly, you're
pretty, and sexy and very, very soft to hold'? Do you realize,
Jack, you haven't told me that *once* in the last few days? And
that used to be your pet line for me. I couldn't get into bed
or out of bed without you saying 'You're pretty, and sexy
and very, very soft to hold,'" Molly said, giving him a chas-
tising look.

Jack felt his face redden. He completely forgot the more complex aspects of their dilemma, overwhelmed by the fact that *was* something he would say. He remembered saying something similar to Barbara. It was uncanny how Molly's fantasies seemed to have tapped into things even he'd forgotten. "We haven't been in bed together recently," he answered inanely.

"I know," she said, then seemingly without cause or provocation she brightened and changed the subject. "Anyway, to my parents, the ability to make French toast is good, but being organized, efficient and thorough is even better. If you'd tell them that the next time they're here, they'd probably be fairly impressed. They might even think I'm making progress."

This time Jack frowned. He remembered the odd conversation about her parents at Mahoney's the night of her accident. He remembered realizing something was wrong. Maybe wrong enough for her not to want to get her memory back.

"Molly, I sometimes get the impression you don't think your parents like you."

She gasped at the very thought. "One of the foundations of a good life," she said, sounding more like she was repeating something she'd heard on their tapes than something she believed, "is a close, loving family. You don't raise children not to like them, or to be critical and judgmental. You raise them to be your friends, your companions, your peers someday...."

"And since you're not on the fast track of success like they are," Jack speculated, "then you're not a potential peer. So even though your parents don't dislike you, they still want you to be someone you're not."

Molly blew her breath out on a sigh. "They've never come right out and said it.... I mean, they haven't actually asked me to change—at least not much." She paused, sighed again. "It's hard for them to be success teachers, people who live in the public eye, and have a child who doesn't practice what they preach. In some ways, I think I make them look bad.''

''My first wife's parents thought children were the result of an overabundance of love. They thought that two people who loved each other made love, and from making love they created a child. Which, theoretically, created more love in the home. Their belief was the more children, the more love. They had nine. Not to create their own circle of friends or to be a foundation for success, simply to love.''

Molly stared at him pensively for a minute. He knew she was pondering what he'd said and hoped it might spur her into getting her memory back. Particularly since she should wonder why she didn't know he had a first wife.

Expecting her to come up with a question about why she didn't know anything about his past, Jack was taken aback and answered without thinking when she said, ''Why didn't you ever have children with your first wife?''

''She died before we had a chance.''

Molly put a consoling hand across his wrist. ''Oh, I'm so sorry. But I'm not surprised you married someone like her. I can see you with a house full of kids, believing that each new child only brought more love.''

Jack couldn't help himself; he scowled. ''Fairly naive.''

''Oh, my, no,'' Molly whispered. ''Fairly wonderful.''

For the first time since Barbara's death, Jack didn't feel awkward talking about having children. Mostly because he realized that if he was going to coerce Molly into facing her past, whatever demons lie there, then he had to be willing to face his.

''Barbara and I weren't kids, but she made me feel young and strong and as if anything were possible,'' he said, voicing feelings he'd kept bottled up because even though they were good they were too painful to remember.

''She must have been terrific.''

''She was,'' Jack agreed, prepared to fight off the urge to

break something, but the feeling never came. Instead, he had a sense of relief and release. As if he had rejoined the human race, as Dr. Tim had said.

Awkward with this new discovery, he brought the conversation back to where it should be. "Why don't you tell me more about your parents?" he said, liberally pouring maple syrup on two new slices of French toast.

"They're two fireballs of energy," Molly said.

Hearing the emotion in her voice, Jack knew that she loved them. Their profession, it seemed, was what got in the way of a normal relationship.

"My mother is dynamic. My father is laid-back, but powerful."

"They sound very interesting."

"Oh, they are. When I was young and they'd host weekend seminars in our home, I'd sneak to the stairway and peek between the banister poles. When I'd get caught and have to go back to my room or outside to play, I'd line up all my dolls and give them fiery motivational speeches."

Jack laughed heartily. "That would have been a picture. But I'm surprised you didn't give the speeches to your friends."

"I couldn't. We lived in the country because my parents wanted their seminars to have the look and feel of a retreat. The friends I had lived miles away. I had to make special arrangements to spend an afternoon or weekend at their homes. Sometimes it couldn't be arranged."

"It sounds like a very lonely childhood."

"My childhood wasn't exactly *lonely*. In fact, lots of it was exciting. Traveling to nearly every city in the United States for book tours or seminars, I certainly wasn't deprived."

"No, maybe not deprived, but you would have had to have been lonely."

Molly shrugged impassively. "It doesn't matter now. But I'm not so indifferent to my past that I don't see that being an only child is the reason I want to have a houseful of kids. Every child should have someone to play with, someone to fight with, someone to learn with. Childhood is all about learning. And not just from books. You have to learn to get along, but you also need to learn to fight for what you believe is right. You can't do either of those if you're alone…or with people who are so much older than you that they're past learning the lessons. Children need to learn together.''

Barbara's ideas about raising kids had been a little vague but, still, it was easy for Jack to see Molly's ideas were more practical. Of course, she'd had reason and opportunity to think her ideas through clearly. Based on her own excellent childhood, Jack supposed Barbara had believed everything naturally fell into place because you wanted it.

Molly knew better.

"Since my parents had always taught me to set goals, I made the goal," she said, smiling, "of having several children." She sighed and her expression became distant as if she were thinking of other places, other times. "It wasn't the goal they wanted for me, but it was a goal. Unfortunately, even that failed," she said softly, and for a second Jack stared at her, wondering if she hadn't gotten her memory back because she was so quiet. But as quickly as he had that thought, she perked up again. "Until I met you," she said, and squeezed his hand. "Now my goals are back on track."

"Your goals?" Jack asked. Confusion and embarrassment collided when he finally figured out what she was telling him. Could she have set the goal to marry him?

Feeling a little dizzy himself, Jack quickly ran through the facts in his head. Her parents pushed her to make goals. She made the goal of having several children. Somewhere along the way she'd gotten the notion that she'd failed. Then she got a set of tapes from her parents the same day of the celebration at Mahoney's….

Could it be?

Could it be that thinking she'd failed and pressure from her parents to succeed had caused her to believe she was married to him—and, therefore, well on her way to reaching her goal of having children—after getting a bump on the head?

That made sense. Much more sense than thinking she'd targeted him specifically and made a goal to marry him and have children.

Jack nearly breathed a sigh of relief. That kind of coincidence he could handle. But for every bit as quickly as relief enveloped him, it evaporated. Knowing why she thought they were married didn't solve the problem. In fact, in a way, it might have compounded it. Now, when she got her memory back, she wouldn't merely be embarrassed, but she'd be alone again....

So would he.

Chapter Eight

"I'm not even going to ask you what Dr. Tim said about our sleeping together."

Jack glanced up from punching his pillow on the sofa. Molly stood in the doorway of the living room, framed by the pale light of the lowest setting of the foyer chandelier. Dressed in the red satin pajamas, with her yellow hair twisted into a loose knot at the top of her head she looked worldly and sophisticated. In a sense, she was. She'd seen and done things ninety percent of the population could only dream about. Tall, slim, with the face of an angel and the power of money at her disposal, she seemed to have everything. If it weren't for the fact that Jack knew she was weighted down by the realization that she couldn't meet her parents' expectations for her, he'd think her the luckiest woman in the world.

"Molly, you know he doesn't want to risk your getting hurt."

She nodded. "I know, but tonight I didn't want to sleep together as much as I thought it would be nice to have somebody to hold me—somebody to cuddle."

Seeing the hopeful expression on her face, he considered that he could lie with her on his bed until she fell asleep, but rejected that idea immediately. This whole charade was going to be over and done with on Monday when she saw the specialist Dr. Tim was recommending. As long as they stayed within the boundaries of decency, Molly wouldn't have to deal with regrets. "Molly..."

"I know," she said, holding up her hand. "You don't want to go against Dr. Tim's instructions."

Something about her tone of voice transported Jack into her frame of mind. He suddenly saw and felt what it would be like to genuinely believe you were married to someone, yet have them continually reject you. Drawing in a breath as he deliberated, Jack weighed his options until he found one that worked. "Actually, Mol," he said, "even though we can't sleep together, Dr. Tim didn't say cuddling was out of the question. But," Jack said emphatically, "let's stay down here."

When she remained where she stood, Jack realized his continued rejection of her had her spooked enough that she wouldn't make the first move. He held out his arms to her.

Her face blossomed with a smile.

It took a minute for them to get arranged on the slim sofa. After Molly appeared to be comfortable, Jack shoved himself even farther against the back cushions, but Molly only snuggled closer. With her head angled beneath his chin, her warm back pressed against his chest and her derriere nestled against him, Jack swallowed hard. He'd forgotten how good it felt to hold a woman, but as quickly as that thought came he realized that it wasn't "good" to hold just any woman; only special women brought out protective instincts and sexual urges. And if you didn't get the protective instincts and the sexual urges, then it really wasn't good.

With Molly, it was good.

She sighed and cuddled against him, and Jack closed his

eyes, half wanting to let himself go, to indulge in all these long-forgotten feelings, and half struggling to remember why he wasn't allowed to let himself indulge in all these feelings. He kept repeating in his head that this was Molly and he was supposed to be protecting her, but somehow or another that logic wasn't working anymore. Physical reality was beating out cold, hard logic.

So he kept his eyes closed and looped his arms loosely around her biceps. He held his body perfectly still for fear that any slight movement might trip an already bubbling volcano.

"Go to sleep, Jack," Molly said drowsily, and nestled into him again.

Jack ground his teeth together to steel himself against the surge of desire that rocketed through him, but within thirty seconds he heard the soft sounds of Molly's breathing and knew she was asleep. He sighed with relief, grateful she'd fallen into a comforting slumber, and feeling protected in an odd way because he knew he was gentleman enough not to take advantage of a sleeping woman.

The soothing influence of understanding she was getting much-needed rest and believing that he was on safe ground relaxed him. Lulled by the familiarity of his own sleeping place, he burrowed into his pillow, deciding to give Molly time enough to be in a deep sleep before he carried her upstairs. But he never did carry her upstairs. An hour later when the chill of night nudged him into slight coherence, he pulled the quilt from the back of the sofa and covered them both, then fell into a deep, restful sleep.

The kind of sleep he hadn't had in five years.

The sound of pounding awakened him. He jerked up on the sofa and almost knocked Molly to the floor.

"Jack, for Pete's sake," she said, clutching his shirtfront to keep from sailing off the couch. "What the heck…"

As if the pounding had only now penetrated her sleeping state, her eyes widened and her head jerked in the direction of the entryway.

"I guess I'd better get that," Jack said, but Molly stared at him.

Something was wrong. She could feel that something was wrong, but she couldn't quite put her finger on it. Not sure what else to do, she allowed herself to slide to the floor, so Jack could get up and open the door.

She watched as he picked and bounced his way to the foyer, realizing that, though his feet were bare, he was still dressed in his jeans and shirt from the day before. Knowing that was odd, she considered that that might be the slightly amiss thing that was tapping at her consciousness, but instinct told her that wasn't it. She watched while he opened the front door and her parents entered.

"Molly!" her mother cried, pushing past Jack and into the living room. "How could you!"

How could she what? She thought it, but for some reason she couldn't seem to say it. Everything was clouded, confused. Oh, her mother was still a beautiful blonde. Trim, dynamic, chic. Her black Armani pantsuit was as crisp and important as her demeanor. Her father was still his handsome, powerful self, with the gray wisps at his temples, his magnetic blue eyes and well-tended physique. And both of them were running at their usual fevered pitch....

So what was wrong?

"I can explain everything," Jack said, and Molly looked at him. He seemed frazzled, out of sorts, not at all the cool, calm and collected boss for whom she worked.

"Molly had an accident."

Her mother clutched the top button of her jacket. "Oh my God."

But her father wasn't fazed. "An accident doesn't cause you to get married without telling your parents!"

Married?

"Well, Molly's not actually married."

"Oh, really?" her mother said, but this time her eyes narrowed as she glared first at Jack, who was obviously rumpled from sleep and still wearing clothes from the day before, to Molly, who was wearing her red satin pajamas, who had bare feet and who clearly looked like she'd just awakened.

Molly peered down at herself. *This didn't feel right, either.*

"Our entire department was at a bar Wednesday night, celebrating. Some oaf jumped over the pool table, swung into Molly and knocked her over. She fell and hit her head. She wasn't knocked out but I brought her here to keep on eye on her. When she got up the next morning she thought we were married."

Molly listened to Jack's explanation objectively, but when he was through she got a sharp pain in her head. It felt as if a bolt of lightning had streaked through her brain. Instinctively her eyes squeezed shut and she clutched her temples.

"And you apparently took advantage..."

Odd images flitted through her head. Pictures of her and Jack shopping. Pictures of her and Jack running into her parents' friends. Pictures of her and Jack eating lunch together. Pictures of her fixing breakfast. Pictures of Jack rejecting her advances. Pictures of her friends telling her there were none of her clothes in the bedroom closet...

"Stop it!" she shouted, suppressing the strange images that were rolling around in her head. Unfortunately, *that* was the first thing she'd actually said out loud, and the entire room silenced.

"Stop it," she said more quietly, more calmly, and pulled her hands away from her head. She gazed at Jack. "We're not married," she said softly.

He nodded. "I know."

"But I've been living here for the past three days and you've been making me think we were married...."

"So help me, I'll beat you to a pulp if you hurt my daughter...." Molly's father began, but Jack ignored him.

"No, no, Molly," he said, scrambling over to where she sat on the floor in front of the sofa and hunkering beside her. "That's not how it was. I tried to tell you that we weren't married but..."

"You tried to tell me when?"

"Well, when I first realized you thought we were married and again when your friends were here."

Her friends were here? Had she remembered that? Her mind was so cloudy and everything was so confused she didn't know what was real or what was imagined. "My friends were here?"

"I thought seeing them would jog your memory. It didn't."

She groaned and pulled her fingers through her bangs. "Oh, God." She'd made a fool of herself and all she had were vague images and odd disoriented memories.

"It's not so bad, Molly," Jack said, and brought his fingers to her cheek. She jerked away from him. "Everybody understood that the knock on the head had confused you. It was evident from the way you were showing the house that you genuinely believed that we were married."

"I showed them your house?" she asked incredulously.

He nodded.

"Oh, God."

"Molly, it's not that bad."

She wrenched herself away from him. "Not that bad?" she echoed, astounded. "Tell me, Jack, how many other people know about this?"

"Not many," he insisted. "Your friends...a couple people we ran into. My doctor."

"*Your* doctor?" Darcy Doyle said with a gasp. "Did you ever think you should have called her doctor...or maybe you should have called us...."

"I didn't know where you were," Jack said honestly. "I didn't know how to find you."

"Don't try to tell me my own daughter doesn't talk about her parents."

Molly wished for the sharp pain again, so she could focus on that instead of on her own personal embarrassment, but it didn't come. Instead, a warm wave of humiliation washed over her, as the sound of her mother's voice caused even more memories to tiptoe into her brain. She remembered the tape. She remembered the affirmations. She remembered creating the very images that probably caused her to believe she was married to Jack.

"Son, I'm going to look into this...."

"Stop, Dad," Molly said, waving her hands. To Jack it appeared that she was conceding defeat. Instinctively he stepped over to help her, to comfort her, but he remembered that now that she had her memory back she didn't welcome his comfort anymore.

"I know what happened. I know I'm at fault." She faced Jack. "Mr. Cavanaugh, I'm sorry for any inconvenience this might have caused you...."

"Molly, no, it wasn't..." Jack said, but she held up her cautioning hand again.

She swallowed. "This is really, really embarrassing for me. And humiliating. I would have thought that you should have kept trying to tell me we weren't married, not moved me in with you. This is so uncomfortable for me that I can't see how either one of us is going to get over it."

"Molly, I tried to tell you. But you were so sure, that I couldn't convince you otherwise, and I didn't want to hurt you."

Jack's voice was soft and patronizing. Molly looked down at her bare feet. "If you were trying to make me feel better, you failed." She pivoted to walk to the doorway, but halfway around she lifted her chin and faced him again.

"My resignation will be on your desk in the morning."

Chapter Nine

"**H**ow could you let me live there?"

"Molly, you have to understand," Olivia said, patting the nubby taupe sofa cushion beside her, indicating that Molly should sit down. But Molly shook her head and continued pacing her living room. Though they'd only been talking for a few minutes, Molly had already recognized that she and her friends weren't going to be able to come up with anything to fix this.

In spite of her misery, she'd spent the afternoon convincing her worried parents that she was fine—because physically she was fine—and even talked them into going to dinner without her. But the minute they were gone Molly called Olivia and Olivia had gathered the troops. All five of Molly's friends from Barrington Corporation had assembled in the living room of her apartment to try to sort this whole mess out, but so far everything they said only added to her embarrassment.

"The day Jack brought you to work," Olivia continued, "we all tried to push you into remembering that you weren't married to him, but nobody could make you budge."

"I understand that I was confused," Molly conceded wearily, pacing between her black tapestry chairs. "But what I don't understand is how could you let me *live with him* for three days." And now that she was home and rested she remembered every second of it. The private conversations, the unexpected intimacy, as well as the times and ways Jack pulled away from her. For every bit as much as she realized he had done that to protect her, Molly also felt acute humiliation. She'd practically thrown herself at him.

"We didn't have much choice," Rachel said. "You were so absolutely positive that you were married that every time any one of us told you you weren't, you couldn't handle it. Your face would crumble in despair and you'd put Jack on the spot. Jack refused to hurt you, so he went along with you."

Molly sighed and flopped down on the couch beside Olivia. "I'm so embarrassed."

Olivia ruffled her hair. "But no one's ever died from embarrassment."

"It doesn't matter. I'm not going back to Barrington. I told Jack he'd have my resignation in the morning. And he will. I'll type it up before you leave and one of you can deliver it."

"No way!" Rachel said. "You'll go in there and face the music. This entire predicament might have been a fluke, but it could have happened to any one of us," she said, motioning with her hand in such a way that she reminded Molly that all of them had a crush on their boss at one time or another.

"I suppose," Molly agreed quietly, though she doubted that any one of them would ever get a self-help tape on visualization and create an entire marriage in her head—fancy wedding, elaborate gown and all.

"Then we'll see you at work tomorrow?" Rachel asked, nudging Molly when she didn't want to be nudged.

She sighed. "I guess. But just because I go to work, it doesn't mean I'm not submitting a notice."

"And just because you feel lousy now, it also doesn't mean you should quit your job," Patricia pointed out logically. "You shouldn't make a decision about quitting or staying until you actually get to work and see how you feel."

All of Molly's friends agreed with Patricia, and eventually they got Molly to commit to keeping an open mind about her job. But with that they let the discussion of Molly's three days as Mrs. Jack Cavanaugh die. It was another two hours before her parents returned from dinner, and her friends stayed with her until they did. If these were any other women, Molly might have thought they didn't want to give her a chance to change her mind about returning to work. Because these women were her closest friends, people who loved and trusted her, she knew they simply didn't want her to wallow in misery. She loved them for that.

The next morning, she dressed carefully. The temptation was strong to wear something mousy and nondescript, but since the cat was out of the bag about her parents, and since she didn't want Jack to think she was a coward, Molly wore a flashy red silk dress. She fluffed her hair, wore her favorite heels and marched into Barrington as if she owned the place.

Only a few people gave her strange looks. One or two asked why she'd been out all day Thursday and half of Friday, but basically everyone treated her the same way they normally did. By the time she reached the elevator, Molly realized that the general population of the company didn't seem to know the embarrassing details of her accident. In a sense, she was safe—at least safe enough that she knew she could enter and exit the building without needing a trench coat and dark glasses.

Her steps became a little lighter, her smile a little less forced. Riding the elevator, she felt some of her stiff muscles loosen. When the bell rang, signaling her floor, Molly drew a long breath. This was the real test. Her own department, the people who had been at Mahoney's. The people in whom Jack might have confided.

The door whooshed open and she stepped out.

"Hey, welcome back," Sandy Johnson said with a smile as Molly entered the reception area. "How are you feeling? Jack said you hit your head after we left Mahoney's last Wednesday night. Did you have to go to the hospital? Did you have a concussion? Was that why you had to leave after lunch on Friday?"

Molly shook her head. "No. I was...dizzy," she said, not able to think of anything better. "I saw a doctor," she added, though she didn't say that the doctor was Jack's friend from grade school. "And he told me I was fine. I simply had to wait for the dizziness to go away."

"Well, you look terrific," Sandy said with a sigh, taking in Molly's chic outfit and perky hair. "No one would ever guess you'd been sick."

There. That wasn't so hard, Molly thought. If nothing else, she knew Jack hadn't told Sandy. "Where's Mr. Cavanaugh?"

Sandy's brow furrowed. "You mean Jack?"

Molly nodded.

"*Jack* is out of the office this week," she said, emphasizing the fact that everyone used his first name. "He called me yesterday afternoon and told me that something had come up, so he wouldn't be in until next Monday."

Molly felt her heart stop. "Oh," she said, wondering if he was staying away to give her time to get comfortable again, or if he was staying away because he was too embarrassed to face her. Humiliation reddened her cheeks. "Well, I guess we'll see him next Monday, then."

"Yes, we will," Sandy agreed, as she strode to her desk.

As everyone began to arrive for work, saying good morning and then funneling off to their respective workstations,

Molly stood in the center of the room, her shuffling co-workers maneuvering around her.

Suddenly she got a strange surge of understanding that caused her heart to swell with hope. It was all the same. Absolutely and completely the same. Nothing had changed. No one treated her any differently—because no one knew.

It was as if those fateful three days hadn't happened.

Her swell of hope was unexpectedly replaced by a tingle of regret. Molly grasped the handle of her briefcase and headed for her office.

What a shame.

She'd been "married" to Jack Cavanaugh for three days. In spite of the fact that their relationship had remained platonic, and in spite of the fact that she was furious with Jack for taking advantage of the circumstances, those had been the happiest three days of her life.

Those had been the happiest three days of Jack's life, too, he realized, throwing darts in a neighborhood bar somewhere in the Appalachian Mountains. Snow still fell in this part of the country in March and it was bitterly cold outside, but that chill didn't rival the one enveloping Jack's heart.

He knew the safest, easiest thing to do would be to give Molly a week to get over her embarrassment. So, he angled a trip to western Pennsylvania with Rex Barrington II, telling him that he wanted to get a feel for the area for advertising purposes before Barrington Corporation made any decisions about the hotel they were considering.

The senior Barrington's trip lasted all of two days, but Jack managed to finagle another three days and he'd spent most of them alone and bored—thinking about how dull his life had become, thinking about what a surprise Molly had turned out to be, thinking about how interesting it would be if she were his wife.

His feelings weren't based merely on the fact that she was

attractive—dynamite, actually. No, there were plenty of attractive women in the world. Some of them had even come on to him in the past five years. But he'd managed to skirt the issue of women and dating by more or less becoming everybody's best friend, rather than a potential boyfriend, lover or mate. With Molly, everything was different. They had connected.

But he wasn't in the market for a girlfriend, lover or mate. He'd been down that road once, and the end was so painful it nearly killed him. He didn't want to go through that again, couldn't even entertain the possibility.

Besides, those three days weren't real, Jack reminded himself, throwing a dart that stuck in the wall a good six inches to the right of the dartboard, reflecting his mood, his life. Everything was always off the mark. In the beginning it appeared good, but when the dart landed it was nowhere near where it was supposed to be. Even if Molly did have a crush on him, she didn't know him. Not really. And he didn't know her.

The whole thing, the connection, the intimacy, even the friendship wasn't real.

He deliberately arrived two hours late for work the following Monday morning. When he stepped off the elevator, the entire department was hushed.

Talking on the phone, while leafing through a magazine, Julie Cramer was oblivious to his entry.

Dictaphone headphones in her ears, Sandy Johnson typed furiously.

Her head bent in concentration, Molly worked diligently. Through the glass top of her door, Jack could see her marking a computer printout, her pencil racing across the paper.

Everything was right with the world.

Jack almost breathed a sigh of relief, except he couldn't do that until he knew his desk didn't hold a letter of resignation from Molly, giving him a two-week notice.

He entered his office, found the usual avalanche of clutter and began digging. After ten minutes, Sandy came in with a cup of coffee.

"I know this isn't in my job description," she said pleasantly, "but you look like you could use this."

Jack smiled. "I'm fine."

"You seem nervous," Sandy insisted. "Like you didn't sleep all night."

He hadn't. He also hadn't found a letter of resignation from Molly. Sighing, he gave up the ghost. "Sandy, Molly didn't by any chance submit a letter of resignation?"

"Oh, gosh, no! She's happier than I've ever seen her. Her parents are spending two weeks with her here in Phoenix and she's walking on air."

"Really?" Jack asked, leaning back in his chair before sipping the piping hot coffee Sandy had brought for him. He remembered the things Molly had told him about her parents—the high expectations, her inability to fulfill them, her loneliness. "A visit from her parents is probably exactly what she needs right now."

And since that end of Molly's problem was getting straightened out, and since she was happy, content and back to normal emotionally, Jack concluded they should broach *their* problem head-on and get that awkwardness out of the way, too. Now that she'd had a week to reconcile herself to what had happened and to discover that only a few of her closest friends knew the story, Jack felt she was probably ready to rationally discuss their situation. Despite the terrible way they'd parted company the previous Sunday, they would sort out this problem like mature adults and get on with the rest of their lives.

"I think we should wait until after lunch to tackle this heap," Jack told Sandy, who nodded with agreement.

"I have tons of typing for the creative types," she admitted, then glanced at her watch. "I'd say that two o'clock would be good for me."

That sounded fine to Jack, too. "Great, I'll see you after lunch then."

Sandy nodded and happily left his office. Jack picked up his coffee and followed her, swerving toward Molly's office when Sandy went straight ahead to her desk.

He tapped the glass twice before opening the door and entering without invitation.

"Good morning, Molly."

She blinked a few times as if adjusting her eyes after looking at the green bar paper for so long. "Good morning, Mr. Cavanaugh."

Realizing she hadn't been adjusting to looking up from her printout, but rather, adjusting to seeing *him*—and the result of that adjustment wasn't exactly good—Jack closed her office door. "Molly, calling me Mr. Cavanaugh only brings attention to the fact that there's tension between us. I came in here to tell you that I think we can both go back to normal...."

"Normal?" she said with a gasp, surprising him with the intensity of her response. "I lived with you for three days. You let me believe we were married."

"I was only..."

"Being kind?" Molly asked sarcastically. "Forget that. Did it ever occur to you that I would be mortally embarrassed when the truth came out?"

Jack winced. "It did," he admitted ruefully. "But you were so vulnerable...."

"Vulnerable," she all but spat, rising from her seat to pace. "From my vantage point, I was six times more vulnerable living in a house with a man I hardly know."

Jack wasn't quite sure why, but her attitude got his hackles up. He'd done what he'd thought was best for her. He'd guarded her every step of the way. *She'd* insisted they were married; *he'd* tried to tell her they weren't. *She'd* kissed his neck. *He'd* gently turned her away. All right, maybe he did jump over the couch, but he was gentle in the way he changed the subject and the mood. *She* was the one who kept wanting to sleep in the same bed. *He* was the one who kept his cool and his common sense. Yet she was acting as if this were all his fault.

"I certainly never would have guessed that you feel you don't know me. From *my* vantage point," he said, pointing at his chest. "I got the impression you thought you knew me pretty damned well."

"That's exactly what I mean. You let me humiliate myself."

"Ah, Molly," Jack groaned. "You didn't humiliate yourself. You had hit your head. You were confused. And you were also among friends."

Furious, she whirled on him. "Stop calling yourself my friend. You spent the past four years insulating yourself from even having a private conversation with me. Never mind being alone with me—except in this office, with the glass door, so no one would ever be able to wonder about what you were doing in here."

Jack frowned. Had he done that? He didn't think so.

"So don't call yourself my friend. You're not my friend."

"Molly, I think you've got everything twisted here...."

"I don't have things twisted. I have my full capacity now. I remember the past, I'm aware of what's happening in the present, and I can clearly see my future." She leaned across her desk. "It doesn't include you," she emphatically stated.

Fissions of anger danced across Jack's flesh. Facts and opinions warred in his brain. Damn her. Not only had he taken care of her when she needed care, but he'd endured hours—no, days—of unsatisfied arousal, protecting her even from himself. Now she was throwing it all back in his face.

Remembering the three days of unsatisfied arousal, the feeling of her smooth hands on him, her soft lips on the back of his neck and her rounded bottom curled into him, Jack ground his teeth. It didn't help to see that she was all decked out in a pale blue suit that didn't merely bring out the color of her blond hair and flawless complexion, it also seemed to highlight her nearly perfect figure. He felt the odd sensation that she wasn't merely throwing his friendship back at him, she was taunting him with what he couldn't have.

Holding back his anger, he became aware of every breath that was going into and coming out of his lungs. This wasn't good. It wasn't good at all. Not only was he piqued, but he was thinking of Molly in sexual terms again.

Knowing he was getting in over his head and that they'd do better to continue this conversation when both of them were a little less emotional, he drew a long breath, spun around and walked out of her office.

She followed him into his.

Because he was striding to his desk with his back to her, he didn't realize she was behind him until she slammed the door. He turned around and saw her leaning across his desk, eyes blazing with fury.

"I see you're not done."

"You're not going to walk away from me. You're not going to ignore me. I'm going to have my say and you're going to listen."

He got the uneasy feeling that Molly believed he'd deliberately ignored her over the past four years, when nothing could have been farther from the truth. Yes, she was the one person in his department with whom he didn't have a close, personal relationship, but that wasn't because he didn't like her. It was because…because… Well, actually, he couldn't say, except to guess that the opportunity to get personal, friendly, with her simply hadn't arisen. Of course, he hadn't really tried to make an opportunity, either. So, maybe she had a point.

"I'm sorry, Molly. Go ahead."

She didn't seem to know how to handle his calm response. Or maybe she realized being angry wasn't solving anything. Jack watched as she opened her mouth several times to speak, then shut it again, until eventually she appeared to talk herself out of her outrage.

"I just want to make one thing perfectly clear with you," she said, striding to his door and catching the door handle. "The next time I'm sick, or confused, or even in trouble, don't try to be my friend."

He understood her anger. He understood her sense of embarrassment, maybe even humiliation. But he'd taken care of her, helped her when she needed help. He didn't deserve her criticism, and he certainly didn't deserve to be punished by being locked out of her life.

He also wasn't allowing her to walk out of this room with that attitude. She was an underling. He was her boss. No matter what happened between them personally, he wasn't letting her think she had a reason to fear him—or even to be angry with him.

She would have opened the door, but Jack placed his hand on hers, preventing it. "You know I was helping you."

"Really? It seems to me that what you did only made things worse."

He hissed his breath between his teeth. "Damn you." She wouldn't give an inch. "Can't you give me a break?"

"What's the matter?" Molly asked. "Does it offend you that after four years of being everyone's friend, that someone's finally rejecting you?"

Her statement was a revelation. They *hadn't* been friends in the past four years. She'd obviously wanted to be. She also thought he'd been ignoring her deliberately. Worse, she'd embarrassed herself when her fantasies were revealed. Now she was evening the scales.

"You're not rejecting me for the reasons you think you're rejecting me," Jack said objectively, composed now that he had begun to sort out what was really going on. "You're rejecting me because you think I rejected you first."

She laughed. "Not hardly."

"You're telling me, then, that your illusion of being married to me wasn't based on fantasies you'd created because you had a crush on me?"

"I might have had a crush on you, but that's over and done now that I know the kind of person you really are."

Jack snorted a laugh. "But you really *don't* know me."

"Oh, yes I do," Molly contradicted.

"If you really knew me, we wouldn't be having this discussion right now, because you wouldn't be angry with me. You'd know I let you believe what you wanted to believe because I thought it was best for you."

"Or best for you," she countered.

"For what?" he asked silkily. "Since you're so sure I don't like you, have no interest in you, then what purpose would it serve for me to keep you at my house?"

She angled her chin. "I don't know."

"But you have a guess," he said, because he knew she was feeding herself double-talk. On the one hand, it served her purposes to remind him that he'd ignored her for four years. On the other, it vindicated her to believe he felt something for her and that's why he'd kept her at his home.

She shook her head. "No, I don't."

"Molly, don't lie to yourself," he said, and with one quick jolt, he had her away from the door and flush up against his chest. He looked into her eyes until he saw her register the realization that he was going to kiss her. Then he bent his head, pressed his lips to hers and kissed her the way he'd wanted to all those times she'd tortured him.

Chapter Ten

Molly knew that she kissed him passionately several times during her three days of believing she was married to him. It humiliated her to recall it, so she pushed those memories to the far corners of her brain. As Jack yanked her against him and plundered her mouth, she didn't even think of them now. She couldn't. All she could think about was the feeling and taste and scent of him. Her knees had long since converted to rubber. Her hands itched with the greedy need to touch him. Her body longed to arch against his.

She'd never felt passion like this—explosive, overwhelming. Kissing him was better than her best fantasies. Even though he was kissing her to make a point, not because he wanted to, their chemistry was potent enough to melt her bones, stop her heart and make her forget everything but the man she clung to....

Oh, no! Not again! The last thing she wanted to be doing was *forgetting* things!

Awestruck by the power of their kiss, Molly jerked herself away and stormed out of his office.

Jack wiped her lipstick from his mouth, using the thirty-second cooling-off period he knew she needed. Then he barreled after her.

From his peripheral vision, he thought he saw Sandy giving him a completely puzzled frown, but he decided he had bigger fish to fry and kept right on walking.

"I'm sorry," Jack said the second he closed the door behind himself.

Shaken, confused, Molly only stared at him as she fell to the seat behind her desk.

"That was wrong, but I had a point to make," Jack insisted gently. "That charade wasn't my idea, Molly. I'm not even sure it was yours." He spread his hands helplessly. "The brain is a funny thing. Who knows why you thought the things you thought?"

Oh, she knew. Molly knew she knew. Because she was feeling all those old feelings right now; only, this time they were multiplied by about seven. Juxtaposed with the real knowledge that he was a terrific kisser, that his body felt like steel against hers; and knowing that he could be commanding when the need arose, all her fantasies hitched. If there was a ladder of desire, she was standing at the top.

And through it all—the three days of taking care of her, her accusations, even today's tantrum—he'd remained a gentleman...unless you counted that kiss. Which she didn't. He'd used that kiss to remind her that she was the one who was attracted to him—and she'd helped him prove his point by responding. If the situation would have been reversed, he could have kissed her until hell froze over, and she wouldn't have responded. Better yet, she would have pushed him away. But she hadn't done either.

She'd proved his point.

"I'm sorry, too," she whispered, wishing he'd leave. She needed to think. She very much needed to think. It appeared that she genuinely was the offender here, not Jack. And if that was the case she was in trouble again.

"Good," Jack softly affirmed. "Things can go back to normal."

Fat chance, she thought, but she nodded anyway in the hope of getting rid of him.

He quietly left the room.

Molly leaned back in her seat. *Damn it!* This wasn't working out anything like it was supposed to. According to her parents, the embarrassment of her amnesia had given her the impetus to fall *out* of love with him. They told her to take her embarrassment and transform it into anger, and not only would she have the reason, but she'd have the emotional push to get beyond this ugly episode and maybe even come out on top.

But the anger she'd clung to was nothing but a facade, because she wasn't really mad at him. She couldn't be. He hadn't done anything wrong. *She* was the culprit. In a matter of minutes Jack had seen through her outrage and used it against her to crumble her resistance. Now, she was not only head over heels in love again, but there wasn't a damned thing she could do about it.

"Molly?"

Molly looked up to see Mike the mailman standing in her doorway. A tall, handsome man with green eyes and dark hair, Mike was a staple at Barrington. Everybody knew him. Everybody liked him. "Julie and Sandy aren't at their desks and I have a package that needs to be signed for."

"Oh," Molly said, knowing her cheeks were flushed, her lipstick was gone and her hair had probably been ruffled to complete messiness. "I'll sign for it."

It took her a minute to find a pen. The whole time she searched, her hand shook.

"Are you okay?"

She glanced up, smiled. "Yeah, I'm fine," she said sincerely, knowing that he genuinely cared.

"You're pale," Mike commented. "You sure you don't want me to get you a glass of water or something?"

"I'm sure," Molly said, handing him the signed slip, and more or less signaling by her actions and her words that he could go now.

He wouldn't leave. Instead, he shifted uncomfortably. "Look, I know that the full-blown details of what happened to you a couple of weeks ago aren't common knowledge around the company, but because I go everywhere in the building, I sometimes hear things that don't make it to the watercooler."

Molly's face flushed.

"You shouldn't be embarrassed. In fact, everybody who knows you thought you were Jack's wife and spent three days at his house is sort of proud of you. You came out of that situation much happier, much more confident." He looked her right in the eye. "You don't want to lose that edge, Molly."

What edge? For God's sake, she couldn't spend ten minutes with Jack Cavanaugh without melting into a puddle at his feet. If Mike—and everybody who knew about her escapades—thought she had been happier and much more confident after she returned from her bout with amnesia, that was only because she was determined not to look like a scorned lover or a damned fool.

In a sense she supposed that was an edge of sorts.

And it also wasn't a trumped-up motivator.

Avoiding looking like a scorned lover or a damned fool was what she wanted more than anything else right now.

If that was an edge—and basically it was the only thing she had—then she'd take it.

She drew a long breath. "No, you're right. I don't want to lose that edge."

"Good for you," Mike said, gave her a cocky salute and left her office.

Molly shakily sat back again, wondering what the hell was happening to her. Not only did she seem to have accidentally won the respect and admiration of her peers, but she'd yelled at her boss. In her wildest dreams she never would have even thought to yell at her boss, *any* boss. Yelling at good, kind, wholesome Jack Cavanaugh was almost sacrilegious. If she hadn't been so damned embarrassed, she probably wouldn't have been so bent on making Jack see her crush on him was gone.

And she also wouldn't have taunted him into kissing her.

Which meant she wouldn't be right back where she started.

Hopelessly in love and unable to deny it.

Especially not to Jack. She wouldn't blame him if he asked for her resignation.

Ten minutes later, Jack cautiously poked his head into her office. "We're having a staff meeting at one o'clock. It will only be an hour because I'm dictating to Sandy at two. Please have a short, concise summary of your activities to present."

Still shaken, Molly only nodded.

Jack stepped into her office and closed the door. "Unless you think we should hold off for another day or two." He paused, and raked his fingers through his hair, as if he were completely frustrated and miserable. "I know you probably hate me now and that's okay...."

Hate him? How could he possibly think she hated him? If anything, he should hate her.

Completely baffled, Molly simply gawked at him.

Employing vintage Jack Cavanaugh charm, he smiled engagingly. "I mean, it's not okay for you to hate me. It's understandable." He said the last through his cute little grin. Then he sobered and added seriously, contritely, "I'm going to apologize one more time. Kissing you was a stupid, reckless way to make a point. I shouldn't have done it. I'm sorry.''

Molly continued to stare at the door after he was gone. Two things were very clear. First, he was so honorable, it humbled her. And second, though he might not be too happy with himself for kissing her, the fact that he kept coming in to check on her lifted her spirits. This was ten times more attention than she'd ever gotten from him in the past. And though it wasn't exactly the kind of attention she wanted, it was a starting point.

Maybe, just maybe, their three days weren't wasted after all.

Twenty minutes after five, when most of the regular staff was gone and Molly was about to pack it in herself for the day, Jack strolled into her office. This time he took a seat in front of her desk after he closed the door.

"Still okay?"

"Of course I'm okay," she said, but she smiled. If she was going to push him into admitting their three days had changed his feelings for her, then she was going to do it immediately. Now that she had him talking to her, she wasn't waiting another four years for him to confess that he liked her. "But I'm starting to feel a little uncomfortable about the fact that you're suddenly so interested in my mood."

"I feel responsible for you now because in a sense I was responsible for your accident," Jack replied without hesitation. "You didn't even want to go to Mahoney's that night. I talked you into it. I took you out to that dance floor. If it hadn't been for me, you never would have been hurt that night."

With every word he said, Molly's hope deflated. It wasn't emotion, but responsibility that had him treating her differently. Though it was better to discover that now, rather than three years from now, it definitely wasn't what she wanted to hear. His reasoning, though logical and considerate, stabbed her heart with unwanted reality. "Which is why you took me to your home in the first place," she said quietly. "And why you kept checking in on me all day."

She drew a long breath to stop the torrent of tears that threatened, remembered what Mike said about having an edge—or, more accurately, remembered that as long as everybody thought she no longer had a crush on Jack Cavanaugh, she didn't look like a damned fool or a scorned lover. And she knew what she had to do.

"Jack, let's call our three days together a stupidity draw and forget it."

With that she rose, wrenched her all-weather coat from her coat tree and walked to her office door. "I'll see you in the morning."

Life was easier now that everybody thought she'd moved on. But it certainly wasn't better. In fact, it felt a whole hell of a lot worse because at least before she could hope for a breakthrough or a miracle.

Now she had nothing.

Now she understood it really was over.

Chapter Eleven

"In spite of the fact that it started off rather awkwardly, this has been a wonderful two weeks, Molly."

Molly glanced up from her lunch and studied her mother. They had decided to spend their final Saturday afternoon together browsing at the local mall while her father played golf, but Darcy Doyle nonetheless wore a trim navy pantsuit with a yellow silk blouse and a paisley scarf accent. Dressed in natural fit jeans with a short white sweater, Molly felt one notch underdressed. But she was comfortable, and after two weeks of living together in a cramped apartment, she was starting to believe her parents were getting comfortable with her, too.

Particularly since she asked them to stop giving her advice.

"It *has* been a wonderful two weeks, Mom."

"Great! Let's pay the check and see how much money we can spend before your father gets home."

Smiling, Molly nodded and rose, but as she did, her gaze collided with a pair of laughing green eyes. Dr. Tim.

And right beside him was Jack—carrying a shopping bag.

"Hey, Molly," Tim said as he strode over, both hands extended.

Molly reached out to take his hands, but he more or less brushed the move aside and enveloped her in a warm hug. "You look terrific."

"I feel better, too," Molly said as he examined her face. "See, I'm single again."

Tim laughed. "Yeah, well, I think *that's* a crying shame."

"Mother," Molly said. "This is Dr. Tim…"

"O'Brien," Dr. Tim helpfully supplied. "I'm Tim O'Brien."

"He's the friend of Jack's who examined me while I was sick to make sure there was nothing really wrong with me."

"It's a pleasure to meet you," Darcy said, offering her hand. "Thank you for taking care of my daughter."

"I can't believe I'm shaking the hand of Darcy Doyle," Tim said excitedly. "I've listened to some of your tapes. You took four strokes off my golf game with your message on imaging and muscle memory."

By this time Jack had arrived at their table. He'd walked slower than Tim had, mostly, Molly speculated, because he wasn't sure of the reception he'd get.

"Molly. Mrs. Doyle."

"You can call me Darcy," Molly's mother said as she shook Jack's hand. "I now understand that you were a perfect gentleman and that you took good care of my daughter."

"Well, your daughter helped me out quite a bit. In two days I completely furnished my house."

Yes, he had, Molly remembered. She recalled it vividly, clearly. Worse, she remembered the feelings. The giddy, airy wonderful feeling of being Mrs. Jack Cavanaugh and shopping for furniture. Making a home with the man she loved.

"The only things I need now are towels and linens. I was shopping for those."

Molly gave the bag he held a look of longing. The yearning

sprang up quickly, and with it came a strong sense of injustice. It didn't seem fair that she could furnish a house with love and affection and not get to live there. It didn't seem fair that she could get a glimpse of heaven and not be allowed to stay.

Darcy peered at her watch. "Oh, goodness, Molly, look at the time. We only have an hour before your father gets home. Jack, Tim, I'm so glad I had the opportunity to thank you both, but we have to run."

"It's been a pleasure meeting you," Dr. Tim said.

A little disoriented and completely sad, Molly reached beside her chair to grab her purse as Jack's best friend continued to charm her mother.

"I'm glad we ran into each other," Jack said. "I didn't like having you think the worst, particularly since nothing had happened."

His voice sounded as open and vulnerable as the way Molly felt inside, but when she snuck a peek at him she saw he was smiling—really smiling—and she knew her decision to keep her feelings to herself was right on the money. Though it splintered her heart to realize she'd made no impact on Jack Cavanaugh's life except to force him to buy new linens and towels, at least she wasn't making a fool of herself anymore.

"We'd better get going, Mother," she said, and directed her mother around the table. "Have a nice lunch," she said to Tim and Jack before she strode away.

Molly and her mother paid their bill and stepped into the mall concourse. Neither said anything for a few seconds as they turned to the right and began strolling toward a department store. Finally Darcy said, "I like your friend Jack, Molly. I can understand why you would have found him attractive. I agree that he would make an adorable father."

Molly drew a deep breath. "But?"

"But—and I'm speaking as your mother here, not as a psychiatrist—it's time to move on."

Though Molly had already figured that out, seeing how happy Jack was had reenforced the decision. "I am."

"I don't think so," Darcy disagreed. "I know you asked your father and me not to help anymore, but it's obvious to me that you're still floundering, and I think I know why."

Molly squeezed her eyes shut, hoping her mother wasn't about to say that it was obvious that she was still in love with Jack.

"You put all your eggs in one basket, so to speak," Darcy continued. "And now that that basket's gone, you're lost."

Uncomfortable, because she wasn't quite sure what her mother was driving at, Molly swallowed. "I'm not lost."

"Molly, after four years of investing everything into one project—any project—anybody would be lost until they found something to replace it."

That made so much sense that Molly felt a spark of belief that she might get over this feeling of complete hopelessness. "And," she prodded when her mother fell silent.

"And," her mother repeated, "what you have to do is find something to occupy your mind. It could be work. It could be a hobby. It could be redoing your apartment. But you need something right now to fill the blank spaces. Something to think about, to wish for, when you used to wish about him."

That was the first objective, concrete guidance that anyone had given her. Up until this piece of wisdom, her parents, her friends, even Mike the mailman had missed the real problem.

She needed something to occupy her time...and her mind.

It was so simple, it was wonderful.

And it made so much sense that after Molly's parents fell asleep that night, she considered her options. In the end she deduced that what she needed to do was focus on her career. She wasn't quite sure how, because the advertising department was small and well structured and she didn't believe there was room for advancement.

But she had an education and now she had both ambition

and drive. Staying in the same job suddenly seemed ludicrous to her. She couldn't envision not advancing, and yet she knew she didn't have anywhere to go at Barrington.

A small stab of disappointment struck her. She didn't want to leave her friends, but she also couldn't stay at Barrington anymore. In a way, it was probably for the best because she wouldn't have to worry about dealing with Jack Cavanaugh. But she hated to think that a man was actually driving her away.

She decided he wasn't. Ambition was driving her away. Goals were moving her forward.

Though she'd go through the motions and see Patricia first thing Monday morning and put herself in the running for whatever promotion was available, Molly knew she had to face the uncomfortable truth. She'd only stayed at Barrington for Jack Cavanaugh. Now that he was out of her life, she would have to leave Barrington.

Late Sunday afternoon, Jack arrived at Molly's apartment building just in time to see her stuffing her parents' suitcases into the trunk of her white Lexus. A rush of relief washed through him when he realized that he'd dodged another bullet. He wasn't exactly sure how he would have explained his presence to her parents. He wasn't entirely sure he could explain it to himself. He simply knew he couldn't live like this anymore.

He thought he could handle Molly's anger, and in a certain sense he *was* handling Molly's anger, but the wounded look he'd seen in her eyes the day before at the shopping mall haunted him. He hadn't slept, he hadn't eaten. And, damn it, he hadn't done anything wrong. He'd done nothing to deserve this.

Nonetheless, he knew he was going to have to straighten it out because of the two involved parties, he was the older, wiser one. And Molly was vulnerable. Still confused. If you looked at this rationally, she'd been sick for nearly a week. While she was sick—defenseless—she'd believed she was married to Jack, and he'd taken care of her. It was no wonder she continued to look at him with odd, delicate emotions clouding her beautiful hazel eyes. This situation between them wasn't settled. Not by a long shot.

Jack completely ignored the little voice that taunted him with a reminder of how lonely his house was without Molly, and suggested that her injured expression from the day before was a very convenient excuse to visit her, spend time with her. Instead of paying any attention at all to such nonsense, he casually chose to drive to a diner to wait for her while she took her parents to the airport. Remembering he hadn't eaten since dinner with Dr. Tim the night before, and acknowledging he could finally eat, Jack ordered a meal, commandeered a newspaper and settled in to pass at least two hours of time.

When he returned to Molly's apartment, the light was beginning to fade. Because her car was white, he easily spotted it in one of the spaces provided for her building. He parked his Blazer across the street and got out, now damning the little voice that mocked him for being so excited at the prospect of seeing her. He couldn't deny the jumpy feeling in the pit of his stomach any more than he could deny he had a lonely life, but it was the life he'd chosen.

As for the jumpy feeling, well, he never tried to analyze something that had no real purpose.

Walking toward the entryway, he concluded it was his own familiarity with loneliness that had him aching for Molly. If losing someone she loved was new to Molly, then she was probably in terrible pain right now. Helping her alleviate that suffering wasn't merely kind, it was smart. Because the sooner she fell back into her normal emotional routine, the better for both of them.

She answered her door seconds after Jack's brisk knock, but he hardly registered her surprise. Before he had a chance to check his reaction, his gaze swept over her, taking in her soft yellow hair, peaches and cream complexion and all the curves accented and outlined by a shimmery pink satin robe that unintentionally showcased her legs. The garment was long, nearly to the floor, but because its single connector was a belt, a thin strip of white skin was exposed from her ankle to her thigh.

He swallowed. Without a doubt, she was the sexiest woman he'd ever met.

"What are you doing here?" she asked, not inviting him in, but leaning on her door as if to tell him that was the farthest he was getting.

"Excuse me?" he said, not because he didn't understand what she'd meant, but because her legs had more or less caused him to miss what she'd said. Nobody had ever looked so good to him in all his life.

"I asked what you're doing here."

He cleared his throat. What was he doing here? Could he tell her he was worried about her…or would that make her mad? Could he tell her things weren't settled between them…and possibly give her the wrong impression? Especially after the way he'd been gawking at her legs?

Stifling the urge to scrub his hand over his mouth, Jack drew a long breath. "Actually, there are some work things I'd like to talk about with you, and I didn't think they could wait until morning."

Her expression thoughtful, she stepped away from the door, allowing him entry. Jack felt the temperature increase by at least ten degrees and tugged at the collar of his shirt. He supposed in the recesses of his mind he'd expected her to refuse to talk with him. Or maybe he'd hoped she'd refuse to talk with him. Now he was entering her living room, and she was wearing a hot pink robe—a slim-fitting, form-hugging, sexy satin robe…. He was a crazy man, an absolute crazy man, for coming to the home of a woman to whom he was unreasonably attracted.

Yanking his rational self from its shrinking position behind his hormones, Jack took the seat she offered with a wave of her hand. In spite of her very casual attire, she looked elegant, sophisticated and older. Much older, much wiser, than the woman he'd encountered in the mall yesterday. He wondered if he'd imagined what he'd seen in her eyes the day before, then realized that he hadn't. Healing was a process. He'd obviously caught her on a bad day. Today must be a good day. Which meant he was in her apartment with nothing to say.

He cleared his throat.

She leaned back in her chair, crossed her long, long legs and stared at him. "So, what's the big work issue you and I need to discuss?"

Jack racked his nearly nonfunctioning brain. He tried desperately to think about work, but in spite of the fact that she'd overlapped the two sides of her robe, effectively closing the gap, his gaze and his focus kept returning to her legs. Recognizing this was about as close to sexual harassment as a person could get without actually doing anything, Jack straightened up. He shoved his mind into gear and refused to be a drooling idiot, just because Molly was incredibly beautiful. He knew her to be a strong, capable, organized woman....

"I've come to offer you a new job," he said, relieved that his mind finally wrapped around something solid and realistic and something that could get him out of this—not merely gracefully, but heroically.

"What?" she asked, perplexed.

"I had a proposition for you the night you hit your head," Jack continued easily, back in control again, "but with everything that happened I couldn't ask."

Molly gave him a puzzled look. "You had a proposition for me?"

"You're smart, you're organized, you're capable. I thought that if you'd be willing to serve as my assistant for a few months, we could intensify your training and ultimately give you the knowledge and skills to lead a portion of the department on your own."

"I'd have my own department?"

"No. But you'd run a section of this department. You'd answer to me. I'd answer for you to the Barringtons."

Delight replaced every other emotion Jack thought he had read in her expression. "You're kidding."

"No," Jack said, his relief so intense, he felt he could dissolve in a puddle at her feet. "All this isn't going to happen overnight," he added cautiously, and rose to pace her living room. She had him nervous—awfully, awfully nervous—but he was also so damn glad he was rectifying the situation between them that he had the uncanny urge to kiss her…in a celebratory manner, of course. He remembered the easy, casual way she continually kissed him when she thought they were married. Those kisses weren't passion-filled masterpieces, but demonstrations of affection between friends. He had liked them, really liked them, and he missed them. But at this point any kiss was dangerous. That's why he needed to pace.

"But eventually I'm hoping to separate advertising and public relations. What we're doing now is a stepping stone for you to take over public relations."

She gasped, clasping her hands on her chest. "You're kidding."

"No," he said, and smiled because this enthusiastic worker was the Molly he'd dealt with for the past four years. He knew she was a smart, skilled woman whose enthusiasm was tempered with sensibility. So what if he also now knew she had soft skin, smooth hands, hair that slid through a man's fingers like fine silk.... So what if he also knew she was an erotic, sensual kisser....

Reminding himself that she was an erotic, sensual kisser was the worst possible thing to do. His wayward anatomy reacted immediately to the mere memory of one of her toe-scorching kisses, but more than that, all the temptations tormenting him returned full force. In that second, he felt he'd do anything, absolutely anything, to kiss her again. But realizing that, Jack knew his odd yearnings had crossed a line.

He didn't want a relationship with her. He didn't want to marry her or have the children she coveted so badly. He couldn't. He just couldn't. He didn't believe in the permanence of marriage anymore, and a woman like Molly needed the fairy tale.

He glanced at Molly and again saw the delight in her eyes and knew it wasn't there because she was having wayward thoughts about him, but because of the promotion. What she really needed and expected from him was a solid, strong work relationship.

Furious with himself for being so weak-willed, Jack pulled himself together again.

"Anyway, I'm glad you're agreeing."

"Of course I'm agreeing," she said, her eyes shining. "This opportunity is perfect."

Funny, but though it had seemed perfect the night of her accident, suddenly, making her his assistant didn't seem all that wonderful to Jack. In fact, if anything it was a letdown that she'd accepted. If she could so easily work as his assistant, it proved that she had no residual feelings. And although that was good it was odd, awkward.

"I'm glad you're happy."

"I'm very happy," she said, meeting his gaze, and disappointment returned to Jack full force. It almost seemed as if he missed her infatuation with him....

Which was ridiculous. That infatuation had been nothing

but trouble. Look what his own attraction had done to him. It made him crazy. It actually had him thinking that one of his best, most sound decisions might not be valid anymore....

"So, when do I start this new job?" she asked quietly.

"I'll make the announcement to the department tomorrow afternoon. Your first assignment will be to find your replacement, and once that's done you're all mine."

His phraseology had been the worst possible choice. Molly flushed scarlet with embarrassment, but Jack determinedly pushed down the primitive feelings churning through him from a mere turn of phrase.

They didn't want to be anything more to each other than co-workers and friends. *She* didn't want to be anything more to him than a co-worker or friend. He could see it in the stoic expression on her face.

So *he* would keep himself in check.

She wouldn't have to worry about him.

Molly closed her apartment door and then leaned against it with a sigh. If the episode at the mall hadn't reenforced that Jack didn't have feelings for her, the offer he'd just made certainly had.

Part of her suspected the new position was a way to placate her because of the growing discomfort between them at the office. But, having worked with Jack for four years, Molly also recognized his sincerity and decided the job itself was real, even if the timing was lousy.

But at least she didn't have to leave Barrington, and at least she could continue on the road to recovering her reputation by consistently proving to everyone that her infatuation with Jack Cavanaugh was gone for good.

Even if it killed her, she would keep her emotions in check and her heart to herself.

Chapter Twelve

"With your new responsibilities will come lots more traveling," Jack said as he directed Molly to enter the small, incredibly noisy plane. "And the places we'll go won't always have big airports. You'll be using commuters most of the time."

Molly climbed the final step and found herself staring at the back of a passenger who was stowing his briefcase in the overhead compartment. The narrow plane had two rows of seats, one on the right and one on the left. There was barely enough aisle for one person. Two people couldn't squeeze through on a lost bet. She stopped and waited patiently while the man took care of his attaché.

"You're not going to want to bring any more luggage than you need," Jack continued from behind. "And you'll especially want to avoid carry-ons. One briefcase or overnight bag is about all you'll have room for."

The passenger in front of Molly finished his task with his briefcase, smiled apologetically at Molly and took his seat.

Molly returned the man's smile, physically letting him

know she understood his dilemma, then proceeded toward the back of the plane. She and Jack had seats in the rear, but they weren't across the aisle from one another. He'd already warned her they wouldn't be able to talk anyway. The engines of the plane would be too loud. So it didn't make any difference if they sat near one another.

But Molly didn't care. This was the best she'd felt in years. With her new promotion, her mind was more than occupied. Her job duties were diverse and interesting. Suddenly her career was supercharged with possibilities, engaging, challenging duties and the respect that came with authority.

And it wasn't as if she'd actually given up Jack's love to get all this. She never had Jack's love. All she'd given up were a few silly daydreams. Impossible daydreams. Things she didn't really want anymore.

Molly turned and unhooked the knob that opened her overhead compartment. Jack had been right. There wasn't much room up there for anything. Shifting uncomfortably, in order to be able to swing her carry-on bag to the right and then up into the compartment, Molly narrowly missed the gentleman who was taking the seat across the aisle from Jack's. She noticed Jack had crammed himself into the space in front of his seat to allow the other passenger to get settled first, then she put her attention on shoving her bag into the small cubbyhole.

By the time she was done patting and shuffling and generally jamming her tote into the cubicle, she was out of breath. She spun around to take her seat and found herself smack-dab up against Jack.

She pressed her hands against his chest to steady herself and he caught her by the elbows to assure she didn't fall. Her gaze swung to his face, his fell to hers. If either one of them would have moved even a fraction, their lips would have brushed.

For the next thirty seconds it felt as if time stopped. This was the closest they'd been to each other in over three weeks. And not only were they close, they were touching. But it didn't feel out of place or awkward. It felt normal. Perfectly, marvelously normal.

A flood of memories washed over her, reminding her of intimacy they'd shared in another life. She could see from the smoky, smoldering look in his eyes that he was remembering, too. Those three days had been wonderful. If she let herself, she could remember exactly what it felt like to believe he loved her. She could remember exactly what it felt like to be held by him. To be protected by him. To be cherished by him...

Gazing into his seductive brown eyes, Molly realized it would be so easy to fall over the line again, to throw caution to the wind and give it one more try....

But she reminded herself that she'd moved on to something better, from something that existed merely in her imagination. While she had amnesia, she'd laid her feelings out on the line, yet Jack still rejected her. She wasn't going to embarrass herself again.

She took a step backward. "Sorry about that," she apologized, smiling sheepishly. "I guess I underestimated..." She gazed into his eyes and all the air drained out of her lungs. God, he was gorgeous, and so damned sweet and sincere...but he was also off-limits. "...how much room I'd need to swing around."

His gaze involuntarily fell to her lips. "Yeah, I guess we both underestimated..." When he brought his gaze back to hers, the look he gave her was filled with confusion. "...how much space we'd need."

Hurrying to take her seat, Molly reminded herself how it felt to be embarrassed in front of her parents. To be uncomfortable around her friends. To be cautious around every damned person in the department, and at Barrington as a whole, because she didn't know who knew, who suspected, or who might some day find out that she'd virtually thrown herself at Jack Cavanaugh for three days, but he didn't want her.

And she told herself that not having a crush on Jack Cavanaugh was the best, the absolute best, thing that had ever happened to her.

Jack, however, wasn't entirely sure he agreed. Oh, he didn't want to pursue a relationship. He couldn't take another ending. Still, he didn't believe that what he was feeling right now was "the best" thing that had ever happened to him.

But he did know that Molly had a lot of potential and that he'd already done enough damage to her life by thinking he was helping her when he wasn't....

So, as far as he was concerned, this relationship was staying aboveboard.

Molly passed the time of the bumpy flight by organizing her schedule for the next week. Jack stared out the window, analyzing a new advertising campaign, picking it apart in his brain, even editing copy that hadn't yet been written...because now, when he wrote it, it would be perfect.

They deplaned companionably, got their rental car and headed for the hotel. Because it was already five-thirty, Jack suggested they take an hour to freshen up and then meet in the hotel restaurant for dinner.

For Molly, the hour was enough time to indulge herself in a soothing bubble bath, redo her hair and makeup, and change into jeans and a sweater. She'd noticed from the guests coming out of the restaurant that dress seemed to be informal and she welcomed the opportunity to lose her high heels and white wool suit.

When she met Jack in the lobby, he had also changed into jeans and a polo shirt. He smiled. "I see you didn't take long to settle in to the drill."

"What drill?"

"Most of the people I've ever traveled with grew weary

of being in a suit all day and they brought a pair of jeans for dinner.''

"From the people I saw coming out of the restaurant, the dress code seemed a little relaxed.''

"It is. This is a very comfortable hotel, in a very friendly little city, I think you're going to enjoy it here.''

Molly nodded and Jack directed her to enter the restaurant before him. They were seated, ordered dinner and ate as if they were any two people employed by the same company traveling together.

Things went so well that when Jack suggested they continue their conversation at one of the comfortable seating arrangements in the lounge, Molly agreed.

"I have to admit I was shocked to find out about your parents,'' Jack said after their waiter had deposited their drinks and walked away.

"Why?''

"I never would have guessed you came from such a public background.''

"Because I'm a private person?''

There was no way around the truth, so Jack didn't try to avoid it. "Yes.''

"Actually, I've always wanted to be liked, respected and even successful because of things *I* did. Not because of my parents, or their influence.''

"Can't fault you for that,'' Jack agreed, settling comfortably on the sofa. "My father was a pretty big deal in real estate. He cast a giant shadow, so it wasn't long after college before I recognized that I'd never really know if I'd succeeded on my own merit or because of my father's name unless I took a different career path.''

"No kidding?'' Molly asked, realizing this was the first piece of personal trivia he'd ever told her—or anyone for all she knew. "You were in real estate?''

"I'd like to think I had the potential to give the Donald Trumps of the world a run for their money."

Curious, Molly stared at him for a few seconds before she asked, "You regret leaving?"

He shook his head. "No, because I still dabble. I'm in far enough to have some terrific investments and not so far that I'll lose everything if a decision I make doesn't pan out."

"That's sensible," Molly agreed thoughtfully, but she was hungry for more. Anything. Finding out that his first love was real estate proved how little she knew about him. "How about brothers and sisters.... Do you have any?"

"Only seven," Jack said, then he laughed.

"Seven?" She gasped in complete amazement.

"Yeah, but Dr. Tim's like a brother, too. So in a way I have eight. With spouses and kids, there are nearly thirty of us."

"My God" was all she could say.

"Christmas is interesting," he said, laughter in his voice.

"I can't even imagine it."

"If you promise not to take this the wrong way," Jack ventured uncertainly. "I'd love to show you a holiday at my parents' house."

"I'd love to see one," she said, still astonished. "I can't believe this. Seven brothers and sisters. You must not have ever felt alone."

But he had. He'd spent the past five years alone, angry and confused. Very confused. To hide his mixed-up emotions and avoid inadvertently hurting anyone, he insulated himself from real conversation, which made him even more alone. Funny, that the first person he chose to open up to was Molly... But, maybe it wasn't so unusual after all. He knew she was as vulnerable as he was.

"My brothers and sisters are what I call perfect people. We went to college, studied hard, chose careers that could show-case our abilities, and when the time was right we all married well," he said, baring feelings that he'd buried because they were unfair. "Except my wife died in a car accident, while everyone else went on to the next step. They all started families. When Barbara died, everybody wanted to be there for me, but I didn't want to impose my misery on them. I was also a little jealous, a little angry and puzzled that I could feel those things for people I loved. So I shut down. I haven't been a part of my family for the past five years. Oh, I went to picnics and holidays dinners and even anniversary bashes, but I pretty much kept to myself. I didn't realize what a mistake it had been until...until...well, until just now."

"So, are you going to call one of them or maybe have a little picnic and try to make it up to everyone?" Molly asked cunningly.

"If I don't, are you going to shoot me?"

"Nah, maybe haunt you, pester you or drive you crazy, but not shoot you."

Staring down at his half-finished beer, Jack chuckled. Strange thoughts danced around in his head. For one thing, he wondered if he hadn't had the sixth sense that Molly would force him to open up, and that's why he'd inadvertently avoided her for the past four years. For another, he thought it odd that she was the one person in his department he hadn't done anything for, yet she was the one he felt closest to. For another, he was passionately glad he'd met her, passionately glad she wasn't angry with him anymore and passionately glad they could be friends.

"I think a picnic is a good idea," he said, then picked up his beer. "I can't come right out and announce that I'm starting to feel like myself, so I'm having a get-together to catch up with everything that's happened in the past five years. But I suppose actions speak louder than words anyway."

"Exactly," Molly agreed enthusiastically, but she yawned. "I guess traveling's going to be a littler harder to get accustomed to than I thought."

"It always is," Jack said, rising. He tossed a few bills on the table. "Come on. I'll walk you to your room."

She knew the gesture was strictly a courtesy from a man who felt uncomfortable letting a woman walk alone in a hotel, and didn't think anything more of it than that. In fact, now that she knew he'd been grieving for five years, she understood why it was so easy for him to be *friends* and why he didn't think of anyone in anything other than platonic terms.

A strange peace settled over her. A comfort of sorts. They could be friends, really close, really good friends, because they understood each other...particularly since neither one of them had been able to open up to anyone else before this.

She slipped her arm through his as they walked across the hotel lobby to the elevators. "This has been nice. Very nice."

He agreed. He also understood that her sliding her arm through his was a gesture of confidence, of trust. Peace rippled through him. Not only was he finally beginning to feel like he'd reentered the land of the living, but he was abundantly glad that, after everything he and Molly had been through, they could be friends.

They repeated the pattern the following day. From nine to five, they conducted business. Then they returned to the hotel, changed clothes, ate dinner and talked.

The next week, when they took a another trip to the Midwest, they followed the same routine. After three extended after-dinner conversations and six punishing layovers waiting for commuters, there wasn't a question Jack felt uncomfortable asking.

"So, no serious boyfriends? At all? Ever?"

"One. Junior year of college," Molly answered, chagrin obvious in her tone of voice. "Same story as about fifty thousand other women. I fell in love. He didn't."

"Junior year of college you're still fairly young," Jack said companionably, and sipped his beer.

"Yeah, but this guy dumped me, found out that my parents

weren't merely wealthy but they were celebrities of sorts, and tried to get me back.''

"And you told him where to go," Jack guessed, grinning.

Molly sighed, then grimaced. "No. I liked him so much I didn't care that I knew he wanted me back because of my parents.''

"Ouch.''

"It wasn't ouch time until I caught him in bed with a perky little freshman.''

"Then you told him where to go.''

"Yeah, but not until after I made a complete fool of myself.''

"Molly, Molly, Molly," Jack said, shaking his head. "Everybody makes a complete fool of himself at least once in his life.''

She shrugged. "I suppose.''

"And now you're on the path to redemption. Things are going so well that two years from now you'll be the boss. I'll probably be answering to you.''

"Yeah, right.''

"No. I mean that. You're very good. You're intuitive about this work, and that's not just a plus, it's essential. You have a knack, a gift. I'm very proud of you.''

"Thanks," Molly said, proud of herself, too. She didn't know about someday being Jack's boss but she did agree that she was intuitive. In fact, she couldn't help but wonder if she wasn't drawn to Jack because she knew he could bring out the best in her. She might not marry him. They'd probably never have kids. But they truly were destined to be friends, and they truly did bring out the best in one another.

As had become their custom, Jack walked her to her room that night. She'd looped her arm through his as she always did, and they walked slowly, talking as they strolled down the hall to her doorway.

She used her key to open the door, then, smiling up at him, she thanked him for dinner.

But then the strangest thing happened. He bent slightly, brushed his lips against hers, turned and walked down the hall to the elevator.

Molly slipped into her room, closed the door and leaned against it. Her heart pounded, and without any thought at all she could feel the jolt of heat that sizzled through her from a mere sweep of his lips across hers.

What was that?

For a good two minutes, she rested against her door, confused and not afraid to admit it. Because the kiss was fast and simple and nearly passionless—except for the jolt of electricity she got—Molly decided it was a kiss between friends.

Later, she *knew* it was a kiss between friends because he repeated it the next trip. He brushed his lips across hers gently, quickly, and then he walked away.

And it was in that second that she knew they hadn't simply become friends. They were best friends.

Because you couldn't kiss just anybody and expect them not to get the wrong idea. But Molly certainly didn't have the wrong idea. She knew he'd been pining for his wife for five years. She knew he'd pined so hard and so long he'd nearly alienated himself from his family. She knew he needed a friend more than he needed a lover. So, when he kissed her, he'd kissed a friend. That's why the kisses were so brief and so gentle.

Her emotions jumbled and muddled, she closed the door. On the one hand she was oddly satisfied to know that her amnesia hadn't ruined what was turning out to be a wonderful friendship, and on the other she was almost driven to tears that she couldn't have him—not in the way she wanted.

She wasn't sure anybody could. But she knew he'd taken *her* out of the running when he turned her into his best friend.

Chapter Thirteen

"*This* is confusing," Olivia said as she set an interoffice memorandum down on the round table of the break room for everyone to see. But nobody had to look at it. The second they saw the signature, everyone knew what the memo contained: an invitation to a party in honor of Sophia's promotion to executive secretary to Rex Barrington III—a man who'd never even set foot on Barrington Corporation soil, let alone actually done a day of work there.

"Confusing isn't half the word!" Sophia said, falling to the last empty chair at the table, causing her medium-length curly blond hair to bounce. "Imagine how I felt," she continued in dismay. "Rex II calls me in, tells me I'm being promoted to executive secretary to his son, whom I have never even met, and then tells me that he's hosting a party to celebrate my promotion because it's the sort of thing Jack Cavanaugh would do."

Though everyone was engrossed in hearing Sophia's story, the mention of Jack's name caused all eyes to turn toward Molly.

"Hey, don't look at me," Molly said defensively. "As far as I know, Jack simply mentioned to Rex II that our department likes to celebrate our successes and that's why we're so productive. How was Jack supposed to know that Rex II would take the suggestion and run with it?"

"Oh, I don't mind so much about the party," Sophia admitted softly. "But I feel odd—*uncomfortable*—about getting this promotion."

"Why?" Rachel asked, confused. "I would have thought you'd be elated. Everybody knew you wanted this job."

"That's just it," Sophia wailed. "Everybody *did* know. Over twenty people applied for the position, and not one of us was interviewed—not even me. Yet I got the job. How was I chosen? *Why* was I chosen? Did they pick me because I wanted it the most?"

"No, you were probably picked on the strength of past performance," Patricia said. "I didn't have anything to do with the actual decision-making process," she admitted. "But I did pass the personnel files of all the applicants to Rex II, when he asked for them. As far as I could tell, Sophia, you had the best credentials in the bunch."

Sophia collapsed with relief. "You think so?"

"Absolutely," Patricia said.

The women murmured their general agreements as they gathered their things to go back to their offices. On the way out the door, Rachel approached Molly.

"If you need a ride to the party tonight," Rachel said as they walked out into the main corridor together, "you can ride with me."

"I don't need a ride," Molly said casually. "Jack's going to pick me up."

Though most of the six women were well on their way down the hall and didn't hear that comment, the two who did, Olivia and Rachel, stopped dead in their tracks.

"Molly, what's going on here?" Olivia asked cautiously.

Molly shrugged. "Nothing. There's no reason for two of us to be driving, so he's picking me up."

"Your apartment's more than a little bit out of his way," Rachel pointed out. "So I'd say that's reason enough for you to drive separately."

"Jack doesn't mind getting me," Molly argued, but politely, "and I appreciate the company."

Olivia frowned. "Molly, the two of you travel together. Last weekend you took him shopping. Three out of four days this week you had lunch together. Is there something you're not telling us?"

"No. Absolutely not," Molly said through a gasp. "We're friends, that's all. Good friends."

Olivia sighed heavily as if she'd like to say more, but wasn't going to push her luck, but Rachel shook her head and said, "Are you sure you're friends, or is Jack taking advantage of you?"

Molly laughed at the very idea. "Taking advantage of me? How?"

"I don't know," Rachel said thoughtfully. "But it doesn't make any sense. He never even held a private conversation with you until you spent those three days together. Now you're virtually inseparable."

"We're not inseparable," Molly scoffed.

"Oh, really?" Olivia taunted. "Then why don't you ride to the party with me and Lucas tonight?"

"This is ridiculous," Molly chided good-naturedly. "Jack and I are friends. I'm not going to insult him by bailing out at the last minute."

"All right," Rachel said, obviously seeing they were making no headway. "But you take a word to the wise and be careful. You're making it pretty easy for Jack. The way it looks to me, he has a constant companion, a female helper for household problems and a built-in date, all without cost or consequence."

Molly only gaped at her.

"Molly, what I'm trying to say is that you're around so much and you're so damned easygoing, that even if you and Jack might have started something during the three days you lived together, Jack wouldn't have to finish it. He doesn't get a chance to be lonely for you because you're always together. He doesn't have to ask you for help with finishing his house because you take him shopping. And he doesn't even have to ask you out because all he has to do is tell you he'll drive you to every event he might need a date. From where I sit, Jack Cavanaugh's got it made in the shade."

"That's ridiculous," Molly said, and she walked back to her office shaking her head, but Rachel's words haunted Molly all afternoon as she worked. True, she and Jack kept each other company, but that was because they were working together to build her career. It was also true that she let him confide in her. She let him tell her things he couldn't tell anyone else, but Molly considered that part of any friendship. She cherished the fact that Jack felt comfortable talking to her, and didn't let her thoughts wander any farther off the beaten path than that.

If it wouldn't have been for those doggone good-night kisses, Molly could have rationalized Rachel's warning away. But those kisses were odd. Unusual. One notch above friendly, but nowhere near passionate, those kisses could mean about anything—including but not limited to the fact that he could kiss her without declaring his intentions.

When she met with Jack an hour before quitting time and they went over ad campaigns and press releases like any other boss and assistant, Molly felt foolish for even wondering about Jack's motives. He was a man determined to help her achieve her goals because he knew how much it meant to her to become successful. Only an idiot would question his generosity because of a few friendly, sweet, absolutely lovable kisses.

Comfortable as she was with Jack's friendship and his motives, Molly didn't give too much thought to how she dressed
for the party, except to consider that she might be meeting
Rex III, Barrington's soon-to-be new president. She contem-
plated a black cocktail suit, but it was too dignified. So she
tried a slim red dress, but that was a tad too sexy. In the end,
she opted for orange satin pants with enough of a subtle yellow hue woven into the fabric that the color shifted, reminding her of the flames of a fire. She topped the slacks with an
orange satin tank top, covered by a sheer orange and yellow
buttoned duster that fell to her calf. Slit to the hip, it showcased her unique pants while still being elegant.

When he saw her, Jack whistled. "I love it."

"So do I," Molly confided with a giggle. "My mother
would have a bird if she'd see it."

Jack twirled her around once. "Oh, I don't know. I think
it's sophisticated enough that it would appeal to her. By the
way, I heard a rumor that Rex III will be there tonight."

Grabbing her purse, Molly laughed. "I heard that rumor,
too, and I hope it's right."

"Why?" Jack asked, closing her apartment door behind
them and ushering her toward the waiting elevator.

"Because Sophia is getting panicky. She's been promoted
to the position of being assistant to the new *president* of Barrington. She's having second thoughts about her abilities, but
also, never having met Rex III, she's having second thoughts
about working for him. After all, how's she supposed to know
she can work for the guy if she's never met him?"

"Good point," Jack said, "But then again you always have
good points. I'm very, very glad I promoted you, and I'm
very, very glad you accepted."

"Well, thank you," Molly said, but she got a strange shot
of foreboding. She thought again of Rachel's warning, but
immediately dismissed it. A person who took advantage of

you didn't compliment you and thank you all the time…did they?

They arrived at the restaurant where Sophia's party was being held and Jack drove up to the entryway. The valet opened Molly's door and she stepped out, waiting for Jack at the curb. As they walked inside, Jack took her elbow.

Now *that* felt weird. Maybe not weird, but out of place. She wasn't his date—he had given her a ride to the party. So why was he holding her elbow?

In the lobby, Molly faced him. "I think I'm going to freshen up before we go in," she said, indicating the nearby rest room. "I'll meet you inside."

"Okay," Jack said easily and turned away from her.

Molly watched him go, seeing that he wasn't ill at ease with entering the party alone, realizing he hadn't argued and wondering if her imagination wasn't running away from her again.

When Molly finally entered the banquet room, she chose to sit with Olivia and Lucas and was glad she did because Jack had a seat at the head table with Rex II, Sophia, Mildred Van Hess—Rex II's long-time assistant—and several other department heads.

Notably absent was Rex III, and though everyone was dying of curiosity, no one had guts enough to mention it.

"I talked with each and every department head individually," Jack reported to Molly, Olivia and Lucas, when he joined them after dinner, once the dancing started. "Not one of us has met Rex III, but not one of us has had courage enough to get beyond asking Rex II anything but superficial questions about his son."

"I've had dinner at the Barrington residence and never met Rex III," Lucas said. A tall man with dark blond hair and blue eyes, Lucas wasn't merely Olivia's husband, he was also a lawyer for Barrington. "If I didn't know Rex II as well as

I do, I'd think he was either crazy or he made up Rex III, to head off competition."

Olivia stared at her husband. "What kind of a thing is that to say?"

Lucas shrugged. "Well, he's got a multimillion-dollar company here. There are six major departments, and all of them are run by incredibly competent, incredibly talented people. If there was no Rex III, no heir to the throne so to speak, how well do you think those six departments would work together?"

"You mean, you think that we wouldn't cooperate because we'd be fighting for the top position?" Jack asked, annoyed.

"Wouldn't you?" Lucas countered. "If there was no Rex III, wouldn't you be at least interested in the job of managing the real estate holdings of a multimillion-dollar corporation?"

Molly tucked her tongue into her cheek. "Admit it, Jack," she prodded slyly.

"All right, probably yes," Jack agreed, then he cursed. "Rex II wouldn't do this to us."

Lucas shrugged. "I'm not saying he would. I'm only saying that it's a possibility. You have to admit it is odd to have a party celebrating Sophia's promotion to executive secretary to Rex III, when Rex III isn't even here."

"Hey, guys, enjoying the party?"

All four turned to see Mike the mailman approaching their table. All four smiled.

"You're looking lovely tonight," he told Olivia, who blushed charmingly.

Lucas laid his arm across the back of her chair. "Keep your distance, Mike. She's taken."

Mike faced Molly. "You look terrific, too."

"So, I'm seconds," Molly teased.

"No, tonight you're first," he said, and held out his hand. "The first woman I dance with."

Molly happily took the hand he extended and let him lead

her out to the dance floor. She wouldn't even have thought to peek back to see Jack's reaction, except that when Mike twirled her around she caught him in her line of vision.

He wasn't precisely scowling at them, but he was definitely scrutinizing every move they made. But just when Molly was beginning to wonder again about Rachel's warnings, a few people from their department wandered over to the table. Bryce bent and said something to Jack. Jack nodded, rose and walked away with the small cluster of men and women.

He hadn't returned by the time Mike brought Molly back to her seat beside Olivia and Lucas, but Molly chose not to think about it. After all, they were friends. Nothing more. Unless she wanted to get herself into trouble again, she couldn't care about where he was or what he did.

But Molly didn't get the chance to worry about Jack. He returned a few minutes later and didn't leave her side again. Though they didn't dance or mingle together, they actually spent the evening in each other's company.

But the evening went so quickly, Molly didn't notice. She was so much accustomed to having him at her side that it was second nature. When they left, Jack gave instructions for his car to the valet, and they waited under the canopy together, chatting about nothing. He helped her into the car, rounded the hood and jumped inside as if all of it were perfectly normal.

About a mile away from Molly's apartment, though, Jack began to laugh.

"What's up?"

"I was thinking about what Lucas said about the possibility that there might not be a Rex III."

Molly bit her lower lip. "I hate to say this but he had a valid point."

"He had a terrific point. Right from the beginning all of us knew the top spot at Barrington wasn't open, so none of us tried for it. We focused on our own department, division or specialty and together we built a fantastic enterprise.''

"So you think Lucas is right?"

Jack shook his head. "I don't know what to think. Rex II's a crafty man. I wouldn't put this past him." He paused, then shook his head again. "Or something," he said thoughtfully. "There's a reason we haven't yet met Rex III, and I have this unstoppable feeling that that reason is right under our nose."

The conversation ended as they pulled up in front of Molly's apartment building. Because Jack never let her walk herself to her apartment, she waited while he got out of the car and came around to open her door. He took her hand to help her out, but he didn't release it as they walked up the sidewalk to the entryway of her building. He didn't even release it as they waited for the elevator. He didn't release it as they rode the small square car to her floor. And he didn't release it as they walked down the hall to her apartment door.

Again if it hadn't been for Rachel's warnings, Molly probably wouldn't even have noticed. Jack Cavanaugh was an affectionate, sweet guy. Molly herself was a touchy person. Thinking about it, she realized she was the first to start the touching between them because she took his arm walking back to her hotel room their first night on the road together. So she started this. And it didn't mean anything.

And, damn it, she wished she could get Rachel's stupid caution out of her head.

When thirty seconds ticked off without either one of them saying anything, Molly began to feel uncomfortable. Not because they weren't talking but because she realized that any second now Jack would announce he was going. He'd brush his lips across hers, turn and amble down the hall, leaving her alone....

Inside, she sighed. Common sense and intelligence told her things could not be different between her and Jack. The man did not love her. He thought of her in terms of a friend. She was never going to get anywhere with him. And unless she continued thinking of him as a friend she was going to get hurt again.

"Well, good night," Jack quietly said.

Molly swallowed. "Good night," she whispered, trying hard not to sound depressed or sad or even lonely.

Right on cue, Jack bent to brush his lips across hers, but this time Molly raised her hand to his shoulder. She knew she'd done that because she was expecting the kiss and bracing herself. But she also knew she'd done that because she wanted to touch him. One touch, damn it. What could it hurt?

His lips breathed across hers with a featherlike swoop, but when he went to pull away he must have felt her hand on his shoulder because he paused. His lips a whisper away from hers, he stayed suspended for a second before he leaned into her again and this time pressed his mouth against hers with a little more strength than he had before.

For Jack the entire situation had come down to a decision. All of this seemed very natural and very right, and, in a sense, he knew they'd been building to this moment for a very long time. They were sexually attracted, good friends, who had amicably gone through an emotional crisis that could have split them apart. But it hadn't. It had brought them closer together. Close enough that they might in essence be starting a romance.

He put his arms around her and inched her toward him.

She didn't need much encouragement.

He deepened the kiss.

He let himself tumble into the feel and taste and scent of her. He deactivated his brain, silenced his conscience and let himself experience the kiss the way a normal man would experience the kiss of a woman he desired.

Chapter Fourteen

For Molly the world was spinning. Not only was Jack holding her and giving her the opportunity to hold him, but he was doing it because he wanted to. He wasn't pretending to be her husband. He wasn't going along with the kiss because he didn't want to hurt her feelings. And he wasn't kissing her the way a man kissed a close female friend. He was kissing her the way a man kissed a woman he was romancing.

Romancing!

Even the word was seductive and wonderful and sent a spasm of joy down her spine.

She was glad it was spring, glad it was warm enough that she didn't need a coat, because she could physically feel his arms around her. She could feel every delicious sensation when his hands began to restlessly roam her back, as his tongue plundered her mouth. She could feel the press of their bodies as they strove to get as close as two people could possibly get. She could feel everything. Every fabulous sensation from fabric to flesh to physical reaction.

A long-forgotten warmth began to grow in her middle. Her

skin began to tingle. Jack's hands were no longer restless or subtle. As if he could read her internal responses, the movements of his hands became slow and purposeful. One minute, he massaged her back as if lulling her into a completely relaxed state. The next he slid his hands to her torso as if pleasing himself by discovering her shape.

The heel of his hand brushed the bottom of her breast and Molly's response was immediate. Longing spread ripples of fire through her. Her nipple pebbled to life, yearning for his touch. Need weakened her to the point that she had to concentrate to keep from shivering.

As if sensing her reaction, Jack palmed her breast. Rubber kneed, Molly clutched a handful of his jacket. She was vaguely aware of the fact that they were in the hall in front of her apartment door, and that somehow or another they were going to have to get inside, but she was also aware that if she said anything, did anything, all this might end.

"Molly," Jack whispered against her mouth.

She swallowed. "Yes?"

"I think for both of our sakes I'd better leave."

She supposed that was probably true. They'd gone from being friends to nearly being intimate in a matter of minutes. Given their history, his past and her future, entering into a romantic relationship wasn't a decision that should be made in her hallway.

Jack pulled away and stared into her eyes. She knew he saw confusion, desire and a great deal of fear because that's exactly what she saw in his eyes. She could handle the confusion. She could handle the desire. But she didn't care to delve too deeply into the fear. Hers or his.

She drew a long breath and turned the doorknob. "Good night, Jack."

"Good night, Molly," he said, and Molly left him standing in the corridor.

She closed the door and leaned against it, her heart tripping against her chest, her knees shaking and her tummy tingling with need. For four years she'd dreamed of marrying this man, and now that they were on the road to a real relationship, she was scared.

Well, not scared, more like wary. She had the feeling she'd been here before, but it hadn't worked out. Actually, she had been here before—when she had amnesia. That was why she felt as if all this would end at any second, because the last time they'd kissed like this it had ended when she got her memory back.

All she was feeling right now was a little déjà vu. There was nothing to worry about. Even Rachel's warnings were no longer valid. As far as Molly was concerned, Jack had officially declared his intentions.

She stopped the tap of alarm at the back of her brain, kicked off her shoes and started to laugh.

It was going to work. She knew it was! Because now they were friends. Before all they had was chemistry. Now they had chemistry and friendship.

It was definitely going to work.

Jack tried not to think about what he had done, but even before he got in his car the demons of doubt attacked him.

What was he doing getting involved with a co-worker?

What was he doing getting involved with anyone?

Hadn't he had enough pain for one lifetime?

And if he didn't care about himself, didn't he have enough respect for Molly to let her alone?

Or did he want to hurt her, too?

Jack didn't call Molly the following day, so she didn't see him Saturday night. Recognizing that things had happened very fast, Molly gave him the benefit of the doubt about not calling her on either Saturday or Sunday. What happened to them Friday night was unexpected. He might have had plans.

He and Dr. Tim could have scheduled an outing that couldn't be canceled. There were plenty of valid reasons why he wouldn't have called her.

She entered Barrington's advertising department on Monday morning slightly nervous, but happy. Everything she'd wished for was coming true, and though it was wonderful, it also took some getting used to. She accepted her jitters as normal and walked into the reception area with a smile.

"Good morning, Sandy."

"Hey, good morning, Molly," Sandy replied, surprised. "I didn't expect to see you here today."

Molly stopped walking and faced Sandy. "You didn't? Why not?"

"Well, Jack left a voice mail message that he'd be in Boston all week. I just suspected that you'd be with him."

All the blood froze in Molly's veins. Not because he had gone somewhere without her, but because he hadn't told her he was going. Still, though she experienced a few seconds of sheer panic, Molly chose to pull herself together and trust him. After all, there were plenty of logical explanations for why he might leave town suddenly and not call her.

Unfortunately, there weren't many logical explanations for why he didn't call her all week. There were even fewer logical explanations for why he barked at her when she insisted Sandy transfer his Friday afternoon phone call back to her office.

"Jack, you're my boss. I would think you would want to talk with me. You're training me to take over part of this department."

"And you've had three weeks of experience. Three weeks to get your feet wet. Plenty time to be able to figure out what to do on your own."

Molly swallowed. "I do know what to do. I've been busy all week."

"Then why the urgent need to talk to me?" he demanded angrily.

She swallowed again. *Because I missed you.* She almost said it. *Or maybe because I thought you'd want to talk with me.* She almost said that, too. In the end she apologized for panicking, told him she was fine and the department was fine, and hung up the phone. When she heard Sandy and Julie leave their desks for their afternoon break, Molly put her head down on her desk and cried.

"Good morning, Molly!"

Molly looked up from her paperwork to see Jack standing in her doorway. There'd been no call over the weekend. No apology. No explanation. Nothing. Which meant he must have decided to ignore the kiss they'd shared, because it appeared they were back to being boss and assistant.

"Good morning, Jack."

In his usual I'm-everybody's-best-friend kind of fashion, he flopped into the chair in front of her desk. "So fill me in on what happened while I was away."

"Not much, really," Molly said, fiddling with her pencil. "I mean, we made progress on all our campaigns. I chaired the interdepartmental meetings. I reviewed everyone's weekly assignment sheet."

"You see," Jack said happily, "I told you you didn't need me."

For thirty seconds Molly only stared at him, wondering if he'd meant for his statement to be double-edged. She considered asking if his behavior and that statement were designed to let her know that the kiss they'd shared two Fridays ago had been a mistake. But she knew better than to ask. First because that kiss merely was a kiss. Second, this situation was worse than her amnesia. It was one thing to genuinely believe something that wasn't true because you'd been hit on the head. It was quite another to draw a meaning out of something that hadn't been intended. Her amnesia wasn't her fault and it had embarrassed her mightily. Drawing the wrong meaning would be completely her fault and it would go beyond embarrassing her, it would humiliate her.

She cleared her throat. "No, Jack," she said quietly. "You're wrong. I might be able to handle things while you're gone, but I still need you. You're still teaching me things."

Things I'm not exactly sure I want to know, Molly thought sadly. But he was still teaching her things. And she supposed they were mostly about herself and how naive she was.

Molly let two days go by before she walked into Jack's office, binder in hand. "Have you got a minute?"

"Actually, Molly, I'm very busy."

"I know you've been busy," Molly amicably agreed. "But this whole Pendergrass thing is falling apart. I think we need your expertise."

"Okay, leave your binder on my desk. I'll review it and write you a memo."

She swallowed. Ever since he'd returned from Boston he'd ignored her, avoided her and breezed past her as if she didn't exist. She made excuses, blamed herself and even defended him. But this was inexcusable, and obvious. The man was supposed to be teaching her, yet he wouldn't even stay in the same room with her unless he had to.

"Jack, it's always much better if I'm with you while you evaluate something. I like to hear your entire thought process—the bad and the good—so that I understand both sides of how you made a decision."

"We don't have the luxury of that kind of time anymore, Molly. Things have changed. You're going to be on your own a lot sooner than we thought."

"That's a good thing," Molly said, slowly sliding farther into his office because she would have this discussion, not be brushed aside. "Because I *want* the responsibility. I even think I'm ready for it. But I felt I was learning so much more when we were working together."

"What we had was two people doing one job," Jack contradicted, rising. He walked around the front of his desk, took Molly's elbow and guided her around toward his office door. "And that's not bad for a few weeks. But your training time is over, Molly. Now you either sink or swim."

"But..."

"Molly, if you can't take the heat, get out of the kitchen."

Molly's chin lifted. Essentially he was telling her that he didn't want to spend time with her anymore. Maybe even that he couldn't stand to be around her.

Had she offended him?

Oh, God! Maybe that whole Friday-night kiss had been another one of her delusions. Maybe he hadn't been kissing her at all. Maybe the whole thing had been one-sided, but she hadn't noticed because she wanted it so badly. Maybe she'd kissed him like a wanton, and *imagined* he was kissing her back!

As he tried to push her out the door, Molly dug her heels in and stopped them both. "Wait, Jack," she said, mortification spreading through her when she realized that the reason he might be running from her was because she'd misinterpreted everything...again!

"God, this is so embarrassing," she said, combing her fingers through her hair. "But I guess I owe you an apology."

"Molly, you don't owe me anything," Jack argued, and began leading her out of his office again.

She dug in her heels again. "Yes, I do. If I misinterpreted..."

"You didn't misinterpret anything. You didn't *do* anything," he said, sounding angry now. This time when he started pushing her out of his office, she let him. "All I'm trying to tell you is that we don't have any more spare time. Can't you leave it at that?"

With that he got Molly out of his office and closed the door. Not thinking of how confused she'd looked, or how unfair this whole thing was to her, Jack strode to his desk. He poured his attention into the mounting stack of work on his desk, but the blue of her binder caught his peripheral vision and wouldn't let him go.

After ten minutes of trying to ignore the unignorable, Jack finally reached over and took her blue book. Unable to help himself, he sniffed it, and sure enough it held the scent of Molly's cologne. He closed his eyes. Savored. Then held the cool vinyl binder to his cheek.

What in the hell was he going to do about her?

At the pizza party, when she hit her head and got amnesia, he had been determined to make her his friend, but he'd failed. Then he thought accommodating her amnesia would endear her to him, but that failed miserably and almost caused her to hate him. Then he thought the extra time they spent together with her as his assistant would bring them into a close friendship, but that failed in the worst possible way.

Because he'd kissed her. He'd really kissed her. In spite of the fact that he knew it was wrong, he'd kissed her.

And now nothing, absolutely nothing could be the same.

"Okay, people, listen up," Jack said from his position at the head of the conference room table. They'd held a very successful weekly meeting. Every section of the advertising department was operating like a well-oiled machine. Even Molly's assignments were right on target. Despite his ignoring her, she was handling things like a champ. He got a surge of damaged male pride that she truly didn't need him, but reminded himself that that was for the best.

Now all he had to do was make a few closing statements, give everyone a little encouragement and get them on their way.

"Everything we're doing is exactly on schedule, but I had

hoped we could have at least had the Trenton and Boston projects running ahead of our timetable to give us a cushion.''

The group broke into a disgruntled rumble.

''I know that it seems like I expect a lot, so I'm going to ask a favor. Instead of standing at the watercooler, speculating about Rex III, use that time to push this department ahead of schedule again.''

Though most of his team broke into a chagrined laughter over being forced to admit they, like most departments, spent a little too much of their recent time theorizing about ''The Third,'' Jack saw that Molly's face turned beet red. Noticing that forced him to remember their private conversations about Rex III, and that tripped the memory of that one fantastic kiss. Almost without warning, it stole through his system like a thief on a mission. Before he realized what was happening, Jack needed a deep breath to steady himself.

''That's all. Meeting adjourned,'' he said quickly and began to gather his things.

''I'll get that,'' Molly said, nudging his hands away.

Because her position had started out as being his assistant, she was always jumping in, trying to do things for him, but Jack didn't want her to. She was ready to take over the greater responsibility that had been their true target, but more than that he couldn't handle being around her anymore.

''No. Forget it,'' he argued. ''I'll do this.''

''I said I'd get it,'' Molly insisted, sweeping a spiral-bound report from his hands and stacking it on the pile in front of her.

But when she reached for the next item to be gathered, Jack had already lunged for it. Their hands didn't really do much more than brush, but, as they did, a current of electricity ran up Jack's arm. He stopped the ludicrous game of trying to beat her to the punch at straightening up and took two paces back.

This was getting ridiculous.

Because he was to the left and slightly behind her, Jack observed her as she gathered the weekly reports. Her neat hands with the well-painted nails worked swiftly. He studied her hands, noted the way her loose yellow hair swung as she assembled the collection in front of her, and let his eyes roam along the slope of her back and down her legs.

God, she had great legs.

He took a long breath trying to stifle the deep, passionate yearning that filled him. What the hell was wrong with him? He couldn't understand what it was between the two of them that kept drawing them into the kind of relationship that neither one of them needed. They needed to be friends. They needed to be able to work together. They didn't need to be lovers.

So why did he want it so badly, then?

Even as he realized the last, he also understood why he'd been like a bear with a thorn in its paw lately, and why, also, he couldn't be in the same room with her. He kept trying to convince himself that he didn't want her, didn't want to curl up beside her in bed at night, didn't want to make love to her until his muscles were screaming for rest. But the truth of the matter was, he did want her. He really, really, really wanted her. But he also knew it wouldn't work. Office romances never worked. Which meant that even experimenting wasn't fair.

And since he'd experimented the night he kissed her, he probably owed *her* an apology.

"Hey, Molly," Jack called softly, then held his breath waiting for her to glance over at him.

"Yes?"

"You know the other day, when you tried to apologize to me?"

Swallowing, she nodded.

"Well, you didn't have anything to apologize for. I did."

He watched her absorb that. Watched as her tongue ran

along the rim of her smooth lips. "Maybe neither one of us
had anything to apologize for."

"No," he insisted, because it was the right thing to do. "I
shouldn't have kissed you. It was wrong. I don't want a relationship with you. I don't believe office romances work. I
think they only cause trouble. I do want to help you, though.
I would like to go back to training you. Can we do that?"

She drew a long breath. "Yes, Jack. We can do that. But
do me one favor."

"Sure."

She looked him right in the eye. Jack felt his bones melt
and solidify simultaneously.

"We're either one thing or the other. We're either on the
road to a personal relationship, or we're friends who work
together. This is it. You can't change your mind again."

He nodded.

"So we're friends?" she asked, pushing him.

"Yeah, friends."

"I thought I was going to marry him," Rachel said, and
though Jack sat listening with rapt attention, he couldn't help
but notice that the conversation made Molly incredibly uncomfortable. Rachel, Jack and Molly had left the crowd at
Kyle Prentice and Cindy Cooper's engagement party for a
breath of fresh air, and were currently sitting on the stone
wall of the courtyard of Rex Barrington's home. But the conversation had taken an unexpected turn. With Rachel's sudden
need to bare her soul, Jack finally felt the Fates were on his
side.

"This is Nick Delaney you're talking about?" Jack asked
carefully, scrutinizing Molly's reaction. Again she stiffened.

"Yeah," Rachel said, sighing. "He was great looking. *Really* great looking. And I think I based my whole infatuation
on that, instead of things that genuinely counted."

"That's the problem with office romances," Jack said, in-

ordinately pleased for this opportunity to make his point.
Given that this was an engagement party for Cindy Cooper
and Kyle Prentice, both of whom worked for Barrington, Jack
worried that all the ground he thought he'd gained that afternoon with Molly would be lost. So, in the car he'd explained
to Molly that, as far as he was concerned, Cindy and Kyle
were the exception to the rule. Office romances typically
didn't work out.

Unfortunately, Lucas and Olivia—another set of co-
workers who were living in marital bliss—had arrived two
minutes after he and Molly, kicking his theories in the teeth
again. So when Rachel began to draw the comparison of her
failed romance, Jack couldn't help it, he jumped right in and
helped her.

"The thing about office romances," Jack repeated, making
sure he had Molly's attention as well as Rachel's, "is that
when they're over, you're faced with that person every day.
You have nowhere to go."

"Unless, of course, the romance doesn't sour," Molly
pointed out. Jack noticed her eyes were on Kyle and Cindy
as they moved through the crowd greeting their guests.

"I'm not exactly sure how or why ours soured," Rachel
said distantly. "I could have sworn Nick was going to propose. But instead of proposing, he left." As if realizing she'd
said too much or suddenly deciding this wasn't something
she cared to discuss, Rachel didn't add any more to her explanation. She rose from the wall and began walking toward
the French doors leading to the party. "I'm going to see if I
can get another glass of champagne."

When Rachel was gone, Molly faced Jack. "I got the message this afternoon," she said angrily. "But, if I would have
missed it this afternoon, I certainly would have gotten it during your sermon in the car. You don't have to beat me over
the head with a big stick."

Jack sighed. "I know that. It's simply incredibly bad luck

that we're thrown into the paths of two richly successful office romances a few hours after I told you I didn't want to be involved with you because office romances don't work out."

"Yeah, that's really, really bad luck," Molly agreed, though she was staring at Lucas and Olivia. She had a half-dreamy, half-angry expression in her eyes as if to say she had no choice but to go along with Jack's wishes but she didn't believe his theories for one minute.

"Olivia and Lucas are the exception to the rule," Jack said, himself getting a little perturbed. "And I'm not even sure we can count them because Lucas didn't technically work for Barrington. Olivia and Lucas didn't have to worry about the ramifications if their relationship failed. Everybody knew Lucas could leave any time he wanted to."

"*I get it, Jack,*" Molly said, her irritation obvious.

But Jack wasn't entirely sure she did get it. And she had to get it or they couldn't work together. If this madness went on much longer, he wouldn't survive.

"And if you think about it, Cindy and Kyle are different, too."

Molly narrowed her eyes at him.

"Kyle didn't notice Cindy until she completely forgot about him."

Her eyes thinned into slits. "Are you insinuating that I chased you?"

"No! No!" Jack protested. "I only want to make sure you understand office romances typically *don't* work out."

Molly stared at him for a long time. When she spoke, it was softly, accusingly. "I told you several times already that I understood what you were telling me. You know me well enough to know I'm not stupid or stubborn. So, since we both know I understood what you were driving at the first time you said it, I can't help but wonder who you're trying to convince, Jack, me or yourself?"

A hot denial sprang to his lips, but it wouldn't seem to come out. Jack knew she wasn't confused. He also knew she had a point. He'd drilled his reasoning into her head in several different ways. He shouldn't have insulted her intelligence by thinking that two lucky romances would somehow turn her head. In fact, he knew they wouldn't. Over the past few weeks, she'd proven herself far too pragmatic for that.

So who was he trying to convince?

Certainly not himself...

Was he?

He looked down into her beautiful hazel eyes, the bright spots of color on cheeks flushed from the cool night, the wide sweep of her mouth. One month ago they couldn't hold a conversation beyond good morning and good afternoon. Now they were arguing about relationships, sharing their secrets and dreams and falling passionately in love with one another.

And that's whom he was trying to convince. The God or the destiny that kept throwing them together. He wasn't an unreasonable man and she wasn't an unreasonable woman. So why the hell was this so hard to fight?

He took a step forward and gathered her into his arms, for a few seconds relishing the feeling of her, then he bent his head and kissed her.

As always, the desire hit him like a tidal wave. Fresh, unexpected and all consuming. At first, he merely savored all the feelings, then reality crept in. He couldn't resist her because he wanted her. And he couldn't stop wanting her. It was that simple.

But for Molly none of it was simple. It was complicated and difficult. She knew he wanted her. She also recognized he was starting to acknowledge to himself that he wanted her. The hunger in his kiss was undeniable. But there was also an incredible hesitation.

And that was the part she didn't understand. They were two unattached adults with an extraordinary passion for one another, but he refused to give in. She didn't buy his excuse about office romances. What she and Jack felt for each other was too strong, too all consuming to believe it was a flicker that would die. Given their friendship, Molly knew they were well on their way to falling in love—genuinely, deeply passionately in love—but he refused to accept it.

Maybe he couldn't.

She hadn't forgotten that he'd had a first wife. A woman he'd loved and lost. A woman he'd mourned for five years… Five long years.

He took one final taste of her mouth and pulled away. Molly felt a swell of regret, but she wasn't pushing. Not only was pushing wrong, but she knew it wouldn't work. Whatever his problem, she couldn't force him to love her.

He had to come to her on his own.

"I think that proves we can't work together," he whispered, though it must have been difficult because his throat sounded tight.

She waited. Half of her believed he was a smart enough man to throw in the towel when he was losing the battle. The other half realized she didn't know enough about Jack Cavanaugh to make any kind of guesses. After all, they'd worked together for four years and she hadn't known he had seven brothers and sisters, a big unfurnished house and an empty life because his college sweetheart had died. Four years of believing they were perfect for one another meant nothing up against reality. And she wouldn't be so foolish as to second-guess him again.

When so much time passed with Jack only staring at her in confusion, Molly's chest tightened. He looked so torn, it was painful.

Another thirty seconds passed and Molly went from being hopeful to being resigned. He just couldn't take those final steps and she couldn't take the torture of bouncing between denial and hopefulness. How could she continue to hope that somehow, someday, he'd change, when he obviously didn't want to.

"I think it would be best if I got a transfer," she whispered, swallowing the lump that formed in her throat just from the words.

But if she expected—or even hoped—Jack would contradict her, she would have been very disappointed because he said, "Maybe it would be best if we tried to work our way out of each other's lives completely."

If a heart could splinter into a thousand pieces, Molly knew hers had. Realizing she'd correctly interpreted his indecision, a sense of finality and futility swamped her. He didn't want to work with her, didn't even want to be around her.

And she didn't have a damned clue why, except that he was clinging to the flimsy reason that he didn't believe in office romances.

"I'll meet with Patricia first thing Monday morning," Molly said, her voice hoarse from the effort of holding back tears. "I'm sure she can find a department for me, so that we won't have to deal with each other again."

Chapter Fifteen

In her mind, and even in her heart, Molly knew he was right. If he couldn't take the final steps he needed to take, then he didn't love her and she *shouldn't* be around him. But having the presence of mind to rationalize that this decision was for the best didn't help. It didn't help at all. Her entire body ached. Pain and sadness invaded every part of her. She stayed in bed all day Saturday and most of Sunday. But Sunday afternoon, in her kitchen to get a drink of water, she saw a package from her parents sitting on the table. Reluctant and somewhat spooked—because she didn't remember seeing it in Saturday's mail—she pulled the easy-open string.

This time there was one tape. Loosely bundled in bubble wrap, the single cassette fell into her hands.

"The Seed of Opportunity," she said, reading the title. "Dominic and Darcy Doyle show you how you can take life's disappointments, failures and even tragedies and transform them into opportunities."

Though she wasn't quite sure why, the absurdity of it appealed to her...or maybe it was the coincidence...and she began to laugh. Right on time, as if her mother knew she'd be losing her confidence, the tape had arrived.

Suddenly overcome with a surge of love, Molly sank to one of her kitchen chairs. If nothing else had come of this Jack Cavanaugh fiasco, Molly knew her parents loved her. Exactly as she was. Success, failure or whatever she turned out to be.

Because she knew they loved her, she also decided she should listen to their tape.

"What do you mean you want to transfer to another department?" Patricia asked in disbelief. "What department, for Pete's sake? You were made for public relations and advertising."

"So was Jack Cavanaugh," Molly pointed out politely. It was already four-thirty on Monday afternoon. One crisis after another had kept her from coming down to personnel, but now that she was here she felt as if a weight had been lifted from her shoulders. Transferring was definitely the right thing to do.

"And since he got to Barrington's advertising and public relations department first, it's up to me to find another place to go."

"But why?" Patricia wailed.

"Patricia, Jack wants me to transfer."

Shocked, Patricia gasped. "No way! Your performance appraisals from him have always been superior. I can't believe he wants you to transfer."

"Well, he does," Molly said firmly. "And I'm going to oblige him. As of today, I want you to find me another position in Barrington."

"Absolutely not."

Molly couldn't help herself; she laughed. "Patricia, you don't have a say in this. I don't want to stay in advertising anymore and Jack wants me out."

"That can't be true. My God, you don't give someone a superior rating for four years and then kick them out. What have you done? What could you have possibly done?"

For thirty seconds, Molly picked at imaginary lint on her skirt, then she drew a long breath and determined that Patricia deserved the truth. Over the past few months, she'd become a regular part of the Barrington group. She'd even come to Jack's home when Molly had amnesia. But though Molly didn't plan on sharing this information with any of her other friends because as far as anyone knew she'd lost her crush on Jack Cavanaugh, Patricia was more involved than anyone else because of her position in the company, and Molly knew she had to be honest.

"Jack and I have this little chemistry problem. Ever since my amnesia, when I…uh…" she said, then cleared her throat. "When I did things like kiss him and hug him, and in general put us into close proximity, I set things in motion for us to realize that we're physically attracted."

Patricia's brow furrowed. "So?"

"So he doesn't want to be physically attracted to me." Jack hadn't precisely told her that, but since it was the logical conclusion to be drawn, Molly had drawn it. "Every time we're alone we say things we probably shouldn't say. We tell each other secrets that were probably better left hidden. That sharing usually ends up with us sharing a kiss, and every time he kisses me, he gets mad. He might be attracted to me, he might even like me, but he doesn't love me and…" Again, Jack hadn't told her this, but she'd pretty much figured it out on her own. "And because he doesn't love me, he's awkward being attracted to me. I'm tired of him being mad. I'm tired of us having difficulty working together. I told him I would transfer, and he agreed."

"That's ridiculous."

It wasn't like Patricia to argue. Generally reserved, usually kind, Patricia made a wonderful human resources person because her personality allowed her to get along with nearly everybody. Today she wasn't anything like the Patricia who had endeared herself to the other women of Barrington.

"I mean I understand what you're telling me," Patricia said in a quieter, nicer tone. "Because you and Jack are attracted to one another it's difficult to work together. But I don't think the problem is that Jack *doesn't* like you. I think the problem is that he *does* like you."

Molly shook her head, wondering why Patricia didn't realize she'd thought of all these avenues, but she'd disregarded them because she couldn't take the pain anymore. There were only so many times a woman could be rejected by the same man before she had to smarten up. No matter how much it hurt.

"I'm not arguing that Jack likes me," Molly said softly, trying to hide the rawness of her emotions, and hoping Patricia wouldn't push anymore because the discussion was only reopening the wounds. "He does. I'm sure he does. But he doesn't love me. And he doesn't think he can love me. Patricia, you probably don't know this, but Jack was married before and he was very much in love with his wife. He doesn't seem to want another woman and he certainly doesn't seem to want to fall in love again. And I'm not hanging around like some lovesick puppy. I want to get on with the rest of my life."

"Listening to your mother's tapes again?" Patricia asked, one eyebrow raised.

Molly laughed in spite of her pain. "Actually, yes. But the tapes didn't have any bearing on this decision. Like any good mother, mine gave me her opinion…albeit it on a tape. But I made up my own mind." She paused, sighed heavily. "Patricia, if a man didn't want you around, would you stay?"

"No," Patricia agreed with her own sigh. "I suppose not."

"But you still don't agree with me."

"Damn it, Molly," Patricia said, uncharacteristically angry. "It just doesn't feel right. The man likes you. I know he does. I saw his cheek twitch when Mike the mailman asked you to dance the other night. To me that's jealousy. Instead of backing away like this, I think you should be going after him."

Molly gasped at the thought. "I've had enough embarrassment to last a lifetime, thank you. Just transfer me out, please, while I can still leave with some of my dignity."

"Oh, Molly," Patricia said sadly, reaching for her book of open positions at Barrington. "This doesn't feel right."

"It does to me," Molly said. "And if you were me, you'd be doing the same thing."

Patricia thumbed through the book of open assignments for a few seconds, then she bit her bottom lip and glanced up at Molly. "I'm not so sure I would be doing the same thing."

Confused, Molly stared at her.

"This morning I overheard Sam on the phone. I don't know with whom he was speaking, but whoever it was, it was someone with whom he is very familiar."

"So, Sam has a lot of friends...."

Patricia shook her head furiously. "This is different. This is a woman. I can hear it in the way he speaks...and I think he's—I think he's going to propose to her."

Molly heard the break in Patricia's voice. She knew her friend had been in love with her boss, Sam, for months. "Oh, Patricia, I'm sorry."

"I guess that's why I feel as strongly as I do. You know this thing with Jack could go either way. He could be pushing you away because—like you think—he doesn't think he could love you. Or it could be that he knows he could love you and he's afraid."

"Jack's too smart for that," Molly said, wishing Patricia would leave it alone because she was tempting Molly to try again, when she knew it was fruitless, pointless. "He's too logical."

"When it comes to love, nobody's cornered the market on logic," Patricia disagreed firmly. "I'm not saying Jack's witless, but I am saying nobody's perfect. And I think you're wrong to bail. If I had even one thread of hope, I'd never walk away from Sam."

"Patricia, it's over. I should have transferred out after the amnesia fiasco. Because I didn't, I made matters worse." She paused, thought for a minute, then drew a long breath for courage. Her mother was right. Sometimes a problem is life's way of forcing you to see you're going in the wrong direction. "Give me a temporary transfer," she said suddenly. "Put me back in the steno pool if you want."

Patricia looked at her. "I don't understand."

"I'm giving you my two-week notice. It's time to start fresh. Maybe the seed of opportunity in this Jack Cavanaugh problem is that I'm finally seeing it's time for me to leave. For good. It's time for me to find my real place in the world—without Jack Cavanaugh."

Because she didn't want to have to go back to work in the advertising department in the morning, Molly waited in personnel until Patricia had finalized all the paperwork that would put her in the leasing department the following day. Since it was nearly six before they were done, Molly decided to get everything out of the way now so she wouldn't have to face Jack ever again. She got in the elevator, rode to her floor and strode to her office to pack her things.

Unfortunately, she saw the light under Jack's office door and knew he was working late, but she also knew that he wouldn't see she was there since his door was closed. But more than that, she recognized he wouldn't care.

Well, maybe he would care, but he wouldn't bother her. She was perfectly safe and probably better off to clear out her things tonight.

In the photocopy room, she found one of the boxes used

to transport ten reams of paper, emptied it, took it to her office and began putting her personal belongings into it. She found pictures of herself and the friends she'd made at Barrington—Olivia, Rachel, Sophia, Cindy and even Patricia. She had a lot of fun here and had done some great work here, but it was time to go.

Pressing her lips together to keep herself from succumbing to the urge to cry for everything that was and everything that might have been, Molly continued placing pictures and desk knickknacks into the box. But everything reminded her of someone or some event—and how she'd miss everyone—until her chest was tight and her throat was dry.

"I'm really, really sorry this didn't work out, Molly."

Because Jack was in her doorway, behind her, Molly squeezed her eyes shut. *Damn him!* He couldn't even allow her the chance to pack in private so she could get out with at least a morsel of pride. But after taking a few seconds to compose herself, and bury her anger—which would only make things worse—she said, "It's okay. It's not your fault."

"I feel responsible."

"Well, you shouldn't."

"Aren't you even going to turn around and look at me?"

"Not much point."

"Please," he said, and Molly could hear the real emotion in his voice. This was as difficult for him as it was for her. She longed to believe what Patricia said, that he did feel too much for her but was afraid, but she didn't know Jack Cavanaugh to be afraid of anything. Logic told her he was upset because he'd wanted to help her succeed and, since they couldn't work together, he'd failed. She couldn't fault him for not loving her, or not being able to love her. And she also knew him to be a generous boss—somebody who genuinely wanted to help her and who would regret that he couldn't.

Having put the situation into perspective, Molly completely

composed herself and faced him. "It's not going to be easy for me to go."

"Well, it won't be that difficult, either," he said, trying to cheer her up. "You'll have new challenges."

"Yeah, and maybe better opportunities."

"Maybe," Jack agreed softly, but they both knew it wasn't true. There was no better opportunity for her than the opportunity to be Jack's wife. All she had to do was see him and all her feelings flooded her. Now that she knew him a little better, she also understood that he truly would be the perfect father for her children. She didn't believe there was anybody to whom she would be so physically attracted. There also wasn't anybody that she felt closer to as a friend. But he didn't love her. And you couldn't force someone to love you.

"I hope you understand that I genuinely believed I was going to be able to be what you wanted...."

She suddenly got the impression he wasn't talking about the promotion anymore, and an intense misery enveloped her. He was aching as much as she was, because he didn't want to hurt her. In a sense, he felt sorry for her.

Pride, thick and fierce, rose to rescue her. She simply couldn't handle his pity. In fact, it made her mad. "You don't have to worry, I'm going to be fine."

"I'm sure you are, but what if you can't find a job..."

"Jack, my parents are wealthy. I don't have to be an overnight success. I'm not going to struggle for rent money and I certainly won't starve."

"I know, but I wanted..."

"To be a knight in shining armor?" Molly asked, then she laughed. "Maybe I don't need one."

He stared at her for a few seconds. "Maybe you don't," he agreed softly, and walked out of her office door.

Molly felt the floor fall out from under her feet. She felt her world crumbling. She knew this was coming. She hadn't necessarily foreseen a confrontation, but she knew Jack wanted her out, and she knew leaving him was going to hurt.

But she hadn't expected it to hurt so much. She wondered if she would be able to make it to tomorrow, let alone endure the rest of her life.

Chapter Sixteen

"Look at this," Flora Conway singsonged as she slid a vase of roses on Molly's desk. "You aren't even here two hours and already you're getting flowers."

Molly glanced up from her word processor and stared at the bright red blooms in complete dismay. "I don't know anybody who would send me flowers," she said sullenly as she reached for the card. Then it hit her. "Oh, I know. They're from my parents."

"I don't think so." Flora, a forty-eight-year-old unmarried romantic, continued to sing her comments to Molly. "I took the liberty of peeking at the card and I think you're going to be very surprised."

Brow furrowed, Molly worked the small envelope open. And even before she read the name, she knew who'd sent the flowers, because she recognized the handwriting. Without trying, she saw the words *Congratulations and good luck,* and, furious that Jack could think a bouquet of flowers would make everything better, she grabbed the vase and tossed it in the trash.

Flora gasped. "What are you doing?" she asked, hysteri-
cally racing to the wastebasket to rescue the delicate blooms.

"I'm putting that where it belongs," Molly replied, and
slid her earphones into her ears. But she stopped and took
them out again. "Unless you'd like those flowers. If you want
them, they're yours."

Flora seemed pleased with her sudden good fortune,
scooped the roses out of the garbage and nearly raced back
to her desk. Molly sighed. If she weren't leaving, she'd be
worried about how the gossip mill would treat that one. Particularly since the flowers might have gone through several
departments until they reached the right one because steno
pool employees frequently moved from one department to
another, but since she was leaving, it wouldn't matter. She
popped her earphones in her ears and went back to work,
strengthened by the knowledge that all this would be over
soon.

But when she saw Jack in the hall on her way to the caf-
eteria for lunch on her last day of work at Barrington, Molly
realized that her anger was unfair. Walking toward her, he
didn't actually see her because he was engrossed in listening
to Sandy Johnson. Like always, he'd taken the position of
adviser and mentor. She knew he'd wanted to be both of those
for her. She knew he wanted to help her be successful. She
knew he didn't like the chemistry that kept getting in the way.
And she also knew that if they hadn't spent those fateful three
days together, with her thinking they were married and hug-
ging him and kissing him and in general, tormenting him
sexually, he might not have felt any chemistry at all.

Damn it! Part of her wanted to hang on to her anger. In
many ways she felt she deserved it. But she also knew his
intentions were good. She knew he was a good man... Hell,
she loved him. It certainly wasn't his fault he didn't love her.

Two seconds before they would have reached each other,

Molly knew what she had to do. She caught his gaze and smiled at him. "Thank you for the flowers," she said politely.

"Oh, did you like them?" he asked eagerly.

Love him or not, nice guy or not, his enthusiasm was a little too much to handle. It transmitted itself to her as eagerness to be away from her and maybe even joy that she was gone.

She took a pace back and told herself not to make a mountain out of a molehill. "I loved them," she said, holding her tongue from saying things that kept popping into her brain because she wanted him to feel as badly as she felt.

"Good, I wanted to give you a little boost to help you on your way."

Flowers? she thought. *How the hell could anybody think flowers would make up for the fact that he found her unlovable?* Angry, unnerved, she looked him right in the eye. "I loved them, but Flora liked them even better, so I gave them to her. I'm sure she'll be sending you a thank-you card."

"You gave my flowers to…"

"Sorry, Jack," Molly said and began to walk away. "I've gotta run. When you're bumped to steno pool, you only get a half-hour lunch."

"Steno pool?" Jack called after her, confused.

Molly ignored him and Jack resisted the urge to run after her. Since he was on his way to see Sam Wainwright about a new assistant, he'd merely ask how the hell one of the smartest people in the company got demoted to the steno pool. But even as he walked to Sam's office, Jack began to understand how Molly ended up in the steno pool. He'd made it perfectly clear that he wanted her out of his department and away from him. If there weren't any open positions except in the steno pool, then she might have been humiliated enough by his demand that she leave to take what she could get.

Furious with himself, he slapped the wall of the elevator and earned the curious, annoyed glances of his companions.

"Thinking about something stupid that I did," he explained, employing his charming grin, but realizing it wasn't working. Everybody continued to stare at him as if he were crazy.

Maybe he was.

Without glancing left or right or even up, Jack plowed through the corridor to Sam's office. He kept his eyes on his shoes, recognizing that he sincerely was beginning to act like a man who was ready for therapy.

Once he pushed into the personnel office, he pasted a happy smile on his face and greeted Patricia. "Good afternoon," he said cheerfully. "How are you today?"

She narrowed her eyes at him, then feigned great interest in a stack of papers on her desk. "I'm fine," she replied in a tight, clipped voice. "I assume you're here to see Sam, but he's got someone else in his office right now. If you wouldn't mind taking a seat," she said, motioning with her hand, but not sparing him as much as a curt glance, "When he's free, I'll let him know you're here."

Jack knew enough about the closeness of Molly's friends to recognize when he was getting the cold shoulder, but he also decided that from their vantage point, they probably believed he deserved it. Without another word of comment, he sat in one of the chairs along the wall. He grabbed a magazine and began leafing through it.

Unfortunately, every time he thought about the fact that Molly was in the steno pool—and that it was his fault—he grew tense with self-directed anger. Eventually he couldn't sit anymore and he rose and began to pace.

"Jack, have a seat," Patricia implored, her voice kinder, nicer, than it had been when he first arrived.

"I can't," he replied simply.

"You have to," Patricia said with a light laugh. "You're making me nuts."

"Good. You might as well join the rest of us."

Patricia stopped typing. "Anything you'd like to talk about?" she ventured uncertainly.

"Oh, I'm sure you know the better part of the details. There's no need for me to muddy the waters with my version."

"Truthfully, Jack," Patricia said, leaning back on her chair and crossing her arms on her chest, "you wouldn't be muddying the waters if you gave me your version, because I don't think Molly's version is correct."

He stopped pacing. "What did she tell you?"

"That you wanted her out of your department immediately because the two of you shared some sort of physical attraction that you didn't like."

Jack considered what she said, then shrugged. "That's a very condensed, unemotional version but, truthfully, Patricia, that's about the size of it."

"Yeah, well," Patricia said, again treading where she probably didn't belong. "If you want to add a little bit of emotion, how about if I tell you that Molly believes you want her to leave because you find her physically attractive, but you don't love her, and believe you can't love her, so you don't want to be bothered with her?"

"What?"

"That's what she told me. After I pushed her to be honest with me about why she wanted to transfer out of a department in which she was doing so well, Molly confessed that the two of you shared some sort of chemistry, and you knew she was crazy about you, but you didn't even care for her, so you didn't want her to embarrass herself anymore...."

"That's ridiculous!" Jack thundered. "Where in tarnation did she get that idea?" He narrowed his eyes at Patricia. "Is this something your little group thought up?"

"Nope," Patricia said superiorly. "This is something Molly came up with by herself. In fact, she hasn't told anybody but me, and I haven't told anyone because I got the information because of my position here and I consider it confidential. I don't think she intends to tell any of her friends what happened between the two of you. Since she'll soon be out of here completely, I think she feels there's not much point. I *think*," Patricia said, emphasizing the word, Jack surmised, because she wanted to be sure he knew she was only giving her opinion, "that since she's moving on, maybe even to another state, she feels there's no point in keeping any of her ties here."

Jack was all ready to set Patricia straight about speculating about people's motives, when it finally sunk in that she was telling him that Molly was leaving.

Leaving.

Going to another state.

Not just another department.

He wouldn't even pass her in the halls anymore.

He licked his dry lips. "Why is she leaving?" he asked quietly. "I don't want her to *leave*. I also didn't want her in the steno pool. I just didn't want..."

"To be around her anymore," Patricia finished for him. "I know. Molly told me all about it. She told me about how you'd lost your first wife, who must have been the love of your life and how you didn't want to settle for second best...."

"That's..." Jack was about to say ridiculous, but as everything fell together in his brain, he realized that probably was the conclusion she had drawn.

He fell to the seat in front of Patricia's desk.

"Are you okay?"

Wave after wave of feeling washed over Jack. The most important one, the one that actually nauseated him, was that he'd hurt Molly because *he* couldn't face the truth.

"Jack, if there's something you want to tell Molly," Patricia said, intruding into his thoughts. "You're going to have to make it soon. Today's her last day. After that, none of us knows where she's going.''

When he arrived at Molly's apartment, she was packing. The front door was open, as if she were expecting someone, and boxes and containers were strewn throughout her living room.

''Molly?'' he called uncertainly as he stepped into the chaos.

''Is somebody there?'' she replied, apparently not having heard his voice clearly enough to recognize it. She jogged out of her bedroom, jewelry box in hand, and when she saw him she stopped cold. ''Oh, it's you.''

''That wasn't exactly the greeting I was expecting.''

Giving him an expression of complete exasperation, Molly sighed. ''Too bad,'' she said, then pivoted and went into her bedroom again.

Jack followed her. He wasn't precisely sure what he was doing, but he knew he couldn't let things end this way. ''If you're determined to leave, I know I can't stop you, but I think it's only fair that I tell you the truth about my marriage.''

Molly was furiously tossing knickknacks into a shipping container. She appeared to be paying absolutely no attention to him until he said the word *marriage*. Once he did, she stopped and glanced up at him.

''I thought you lived in a perfect world of bliss.''

''No,'' he said with heartbreaking honestly, then he swallowed. ''Far, far from it.''

Molly opened her mouth to speak but nothing came out. She settled for sitting on the bed as a cue to let him know she was listening. Jack knew she probably presumed he would join her but he couldn't sit. He had to pace. This was the first time he'd said any of these things aloud and he wasn't even sure he could do it.

Slowly, painfully, he began, "The night before she died, Barbara told me she was ready to have a child."

"Oh, I'm sorry," Molly whispered, commiserating.

Jack snorted a derisive laugh and tossed his hands in the air. "Don't be. She wanted a child because she thought it was the right time in her career. We had finally bought a house and if everything went the way it was supposed to, we'd have two kids almost back to back, then she'd be ready to go on the campaign trail."

"The campaign trail?"

"Where we lived, she had to become local district attorney before she could even be considered for attorney general—and she wanted to be attorney general more than she wanted her next breath of air. But, you see, she couldn't admit it because her relatives were so family oriented that I think she felt guilty for having ambition."

"That's a shame," Molly said and patted the bed, a gesture Jack was sure Molly meant to convey that she was still his friend, still ready to listen, to console, in spite of the way he'd hurt her.

But Jack shook his head. He couldn't sit beside her. He still needed to pace.

"So she never came right out and admitted her intentions, but she also didn't know that things she did and other things she said gave her away. She actually confessed to me once that the success of my family would be a benefit to her career. Once she admitted that, it wasn't a big step for her to acknowledge that she'd realized that even before we started dating.

"From that day, I began to see that she didn't love me, she had *picked* me. I knew that there were worse ways to create a marriage and worse reasons, and we were sexually compatible and I loved her, so I thought we'd be okay. But we weren't. We were two different people, living different lives and intersecting only when we had to, or when it was convenient. I got lonely, and asked for more from her, but she told me she didn't have anything left to give. She was busy. And if I loved her I would let her do what she had to do.''

"So you let her do what she had to do," Molly said blandly, obviously understanding what he was telling her.

He nodded, then prowled the room, searching for a way to say what he honestly needed to say, but not finding any help. So he faced her. "The day she was killed I didn't go to work. I couldn't. Bringing a child into the world was such a big step that I couldn't leave it to the organizational chart of her career. I had to know I really wanted a child and I really wanted a child *with her,* or I wasn't buying in.''

"That makes sense. Everybody needs to think things through....''

"Yes, well, the real problem was, our marriage was gone. Somehow I'd fallen out of love with her. And I knew damned well she didn't love me. It only took me twenty minutes of pacing our house for me to realize that was why I was balking at having a child. Somehow in a few years we'd gone from being this fairy-tale, fantasy couple into being two strangers. I didn't recognize her anymore, and there were some days when I didn't even like her. When I realized we were the last two people on the face of the earth who should be bringing a child into the world, I also admitted to myself that our marriage was in trouble. So I called her at work and asked her to come home. She refused because she was very busy. I told her the conclusions I had drawn and that I thought we shouldn't be having a child, but getting a divorce. When she realized a divorce wouldn't merely jeopardize her career, it would also mean her plan of having children would be set back, she jumped into her car to come home to talk some sense into me....''

"And she was killed.''

"And she was killed.''

"It wasn't your fault, Jack."

He turned away again, agitated, angry. "You know, logically I knew that. But I still felt guilty—for years."

"But you don't feel guilty anymore."

He paused, as if taking mental inventory, and his Adam's apple worked. "No."

"So now you feel guilty for not feeling guilty?" Molly asked incredulously.

"No." He shook his head, then caught her gaze. "I'm through all that."

"Then why are you here?"

"I can't let you leave thinking I hate you."

She licked her dry lips. "I don't think you hate me," she said, then she waited. She watched as he searched her face, watched as he fought some sort of mental battle, watched as he stopped—again—far short of the mark.

"And we're still friends?" he asked quietly.

She nodded, but pursed her lips because she knew she was going to cry.

"Good. Then I guess I can go."

"I guess you can," she agreed, though she had an odd sense that he almost expected her to ask him to stay. But she couldn't. She couldn't ask him to stay when she knew she'd be breaking into tears at any second.

He swallowed and turned to walk out of her bedroom. A minute later she heard her apartment door close.

The weight of loss settled on Molly again and she sank to her bed. If he would just let her alone, let her get on with the rest of her life, this would be much easier, because in insisting on being friends he kept putting her through the same pain again and again. She couldn't be his friend because then she would always love him, she'd never get over him, and she wasn't accepting half, or part of what he could give her. She deserved more. Better. Everything. She deserved *everything*.

If he couldn't give her everything, she'd find it somewhere else. Leaving would be painful, getting over him would be devastating, but she'd never, ever settle for half.

In fact, she decided to tell him that.

Chapter Seventeen

In the end, Patricia concluded that Molly leaving Barrington wasn't really a secret because everyone could discover that on her own. She told the girls at Barrington that Molly had resigned and, she suspected, would be leaving Phoenix. Acting as spokesperson, Rachel called and discovered that Molly wasn't merely moving out of town, she was moving Monday morning. When the big day came, everyone took a personal day and showed up on her doorstep, ready to help her.

"I can't believe this," Molly said, tears in her eyes. "You guys shouldn't have taken a day off for me."

"Yeah, well, you shouldn't have kept all this a secret," Olivia chastised, from her seat at the breakfast bar in the kitchen, where she sat eating yogurt. Because she was pregnant, no one wanted her lifting or moving anything.

"I couldn't tell you that I'd made the same mistake twice," Molly confessed, then collapsed on the only available spot on her sofa. Rachel and Patricia were packing dishes. Sophia and Cindy were carefully wrapping knickknacks from Molly's curio cabinet in white tissue paper and bubble wrap.

"Not only had I fallen more ridiculously in love with Jack, but Mike the mailman made me feel that everybody thought I was strong because I'd fallen out of love."

All five of the women groaned.

"You ignored us, but took advice from a man?" Patricia wailed.

"I didn't want you guys to think I was a fool again."

"Oh, Molly," Rachel said through a sigh. "We're your friends. You're *supposed* to be foolish in front of us. That's what friends are for."

"Yeah, well, I don't have to be a fool in front of anybody anymore. Jack came by on Saturday and he gave me his usual speech about us being friends, except this time he admitted that his first relationship wasn't good, it was bad. It helped me to understand a little better, and I accepted the situation. Jack doesn't believe he can love me, so he wants to be friends. But after he left I realized being friends might be good for him, but it's hard on me. So I called his house before he got home so I could leave a message on his answering machine."

"To say what?" Cindy asked incredulously.

"To say I didn't even want to be friends."

Sophia gasped with surprise. "Really! God, that was brave."

"I don't think so," Molly disagreed. "In a way I think it was a kind of cowardice. Every time I see him I want to love him. I realized I can't be friends anymore because I'll always be attached. I don't want to be attached. So I told him I never wanted to see him again. I want to find somebody else, somebody who can love me."

Jack had been shocked to the core by Molly's message on his answering machine.

Logically he knew her leaving meant that they'd drift apart. But in his heart, he always felt he'd have a place for her. The fact that she was booting him out of her heart hurt. It really hurt to be pushed up against the reality that in moving out of his life, Molly was planning to move into someone else's. Oh, she didn't know whose life she'd move into. She couldn't tell the future. No one could. But she was clear about the fact that she was leaving, permanently and for good, because she wanted to fall in love. She wanted the fantasy, the fairy tale, the dream, the house, the kids, the man to love her. Since that wasn't him, she wanted him out of her life.

And it hurt so much that Jack got angry.

Yes, he understood her right to want all of that. Rationally he agreed. But on an elemental level, he couldn't stand the thought of her with another man. He couldn't stand the thought of another man touching her. But more than that, he couldn't stand the thought of another man sharing her dreams.

So he called her. And he got her answering machine. Realizing she wasn't home, he drove to her apartment and waited outside, hoping that he would catch her returning. But when he saw her coming home and he saw that she was energetic and bubbly—happy without him—he lost his nerve and went home to wait for her call since he'd left a message that asked her to call him.

When she didn't call he knew she meant business. She wasn't going to see him. Didn't *want* to see him. She wanted a life without him. And she was happy about it.

And why not? He'd pushed her to it.

"So basically, when I didn't return his call, I think I made it clear that I meant what I said."

"Good for you," Olivia said.

"I don't know," Patricia said warily. "I still think he loves you."

"But he can't show it," Cindy protested. "He *has* to be able to show it."

Even as Cindy was talking, the doorbell rang. Molly

jumped up. "It's moot," she said, striding to the door. "Because this is probably the movers. This time tomorrow, I'll be in San Francisco."

With that she opened the door and three burly moving men grinned at her. The two in the front were so large, they dwarfed and virtually hid the one in the back. "Molly Doyle?" the leader asked around his odd, smirking grin.

"Yep," she happily confirmed, then let the three men in. "I don't know how you people want to work this, but my friends and I are handling the small, fragile things. We'll have them boxed for you in about an hour. You can start on the furniture."

"Bedroom," the big guy grunted. "You take our pal here," he said, pointing behind him, "back there and give him the instructions. Leo and I are going out for the dollies."

Molly nodded absently and turned to walk down the hall to her bedroom, assuming the mover was following her. When she reached her bedroom, she stepped inside and was unnerved when she heard the door close behind her. Frightened, she spun around only to discover the third mover was Jack. Dressed in the bright gray coveralls and little cap, he leaned against her door.

"Molly, why didn't you return my call?"

She stared at him. "I thought I'd explained all that."

"You're telling me what you want. You're not even considering..."

"What you want? No. I'm not considering what you want!" she said through a gasp. "I've been around for four years and you didn't want me. Then, when you decided you really did like me, you only liked me as a friend. I put my feelings out on the line and you've rejected me. I'm not going through it again."

"What if I told you I only rejected you because I don't know how to start over again?"

"And you're coming to me because I'm the queen of starting over?" Molly asked, spreading her hands to indicate the fact that she was moving.

He shook his head again. "No, I'm coming to you because I love you."

For a good twenty seconds, Molly held her breath, fully expecting him to say, "But..."

However, he never said it. He began to walk around her bedroom, picking up and examining her things. Finally he said, "My first marriage was so screwed up that I don't think I know how to have a real relationship anymore."

She swallowed, not at all sure what to say, not at all sure how she'd keep herself from jumping into his arms, but she knew she had to. He might love her, but he had to want everything she wanted. If he didn't, he would only be giving her half of what she wanted and she couldn't settle for half.

Struggling for breath, she said, "Well, you certainly don't do it by pushing away the people you love."

"I know that...."

"And you have to be able to take a few risks."

"Hey, I paid fifty bucks to wear these coveralls and get the first fifteen minutes of your time. I'd say that was pretty risky."

That made her smile. "You're right. Gray's not your color."

"You're telling me."

Jack smiled. Molly smiled. Neither said anything.

Finally he sighed. "So, what do we do?"

Molly shrugged. "I don't know. I don't know what you want."

Jack licked his dry lips. "I know I don't want you to go. I know I don't want to live without you. I know I don't want another man touching you. And I definitely know I don't want you having another man's children. I want you to have *my* babies."

Molly pressed her lips together to stop their trembling. "I want to have your babies, too."

"You're going to have to help me, here, Molly," he said slowly, cautiously. "Because I'm not quite sure of what I should be doing."

"Well, you could start by coming over here and kissing me."

His head snapped up. "You're going to take me back? After everything I've done to you and even knowing my past?"

Molly laughed. "Honey, I'd take you in a paper bag, surrounded by children, or even if you were dead broke."

That made Jack laugh. "I guess this means you love me, too."

"Sometimes I think I adore you."

He closed his eyes as if in pain. "Don't say things like that unless you mean them."

"Oh, I mean them," she said, and walked over to him. She slid her arms around his neck. "Let me show you how I mean them," she whispered, but before she could kiss him, he'd already pressed his lips to hers. Desperation fused with pent-up longing and Molly reveled in it. Part of him seemed to seep into her, as surely as she felt part of herself going to him. When he nudged her toward the bed, and tumbled her to the soft comforter, she didn't protest, but when they rolled and bumped into one of her moving boxes, both stopped.

She opened her eyes and smiled at him. "I suppose this means I'm not leaving."

"Well, *leaving* is sort of a relative term," he said, slightly embarrassed. "I was kind of hoping we could have the movers take these things to my house, so you'd move in with me."

She gasped in mock outrage. "Oh, no. Not again. Not until we're actually married."

"That would be fine with me," he said, then kissed her

again as if to seal the promise. "In fact, I'll take every one of those five kids you want, and I might even barter for a sixth."

"Really?" she said, but she knew she didn't have to ask. Though she never would have guessed it, she had gotten her wish.

Dream man.

Dream house.

And children.

Lots of children.

She'd never be alone again....

Neither would he.

* * * * *

Don't miss Rachel's story,
THE EXECUTIVE'S BABY,
by Robin Wells, next month's
LOVING THE BOSS *title,*
available only in Silhouette Romance.

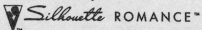

If you enjoyed what you just read,
then we've got an offer you can't resist!

Take 2 bestselling love stories FREE!

Plus get a FREE surprise gift!

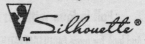

THESE BACHELOR DADS NEED A LITTLE TENDERNESS—AND A WHOLE LOT OF LOVING!

January 1999—A Rugged Ranchin' Dad
by Kia Cochrane (SR# 1343)

Tragedy had wedged Stone Tyler's family apart. Now this rugged rancher would do everything in his power to be the perfect daddy— and recapture his wife's heart—before time ran out....

April 1999 —Prince Charming's Return
by Myrna Mackenzie (SR# 1361)

Gray Alexander was back in town—and had just met the son he had never known he had. Now he wanted to make Cassie Pratt pay for her deception eleven years ago...even if the price was marriage!

And in **June 1999** don't miss Donna Clayton's touching story of Dylan Minster, a man who has been raising his daughter all alone....

Fall in love with our FABULOUS FATHERS!

And look for more FABULOUS FATHERS in the months to come. Only from

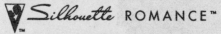

Silhouette ROMANCE™

Available wherever Silhouette books are sold.

Look us up on-line at: http://www.romance.net

SRFFJ-J

COMING NEXT MONTH